LOVE
ON THE
DANGER TRAIL

The woman shivered in the sudden rush of wind that came down through the trees and the Kansan drew his arms tighter around her supple body, holding her securely in the saddle. She pressed back against Davy Watson, murmuring his name and telling him that she was very cold.

"Well, you just snuggle up to me, darlin'," he whispered to the young beauty, his voice husky now, roughened by the surge of desire that had broken inside him.

As he drew the young woman still closer, he caught the fragrant scent of her hair. All thoughts of danger fled from his mind, replaced by perfumed imaginings of desire. He pressed his lips to her neck.

She trembled at first, but then she leaned back, turning her head, and offered her full lips to the Kansan. And as the stallion made its way through the wet pines, their lips met in a long, hungry kiss.

The Kansan #5:

WARM FLESH, HOT LEAD

Robert E. Mills

LEISURE BOOKS  NEW YORK CITY

*To Dave Wasson, my old pardner,
and his trailmate, Susan.*

A LEISURE BOOK

Published by

Nordon Publications, Inc.
Two Park Avenue
New York, N.Y. 10016

PROLOGUE

Shots In The Night

The Kansan breathed a sigh of relief as the thunder of hoofbeats below began to diminish in its intensity. He looked down the slope and saw the pursuing horsemen flash by, ghostly in the cold, eerie light of the moon.

A chill wind rippled through the pines, causing them to sigh and murmur like women moaning in a dream of desire. Overhead, the moon hung low in the bat-black sky, bright and heavy as a platter of hammered Navaho silver. Far below, an owl hooted in the woods, and even farther off, somewhere deep in the belly of night, a wolf howled, its mournful wail ringing up through the tall timber.

Davy Watson hefted the big Walker Colt in his right hand. Then, with an accompanying creak of leather, he thrust the gun back into its holster.

His pursuers had gone, the Kansan told himself as he turned to the young woman who sat in front of him, sharing his saddle.

"We're safe now," he whispered, leaning forward until his lips were brushing her hair, long black hair that was even darker than the sky. "They'll be off on a wild goose chase, darlin'. Now we can git to where I mean to take us."

Having said this, the Kansan flicked the reins and emitted two brief, clicking sounds out of the side of his mouth. The big stallion beneath him snorted, shook its mane, and shot up the slope, making its ascent between two rows of sheltering pines.

The woman shivered in the sudden rush of wind that came down through the trees, and the Kansan drew his arms tighter around her supple body. She leaned back against Davy, murmuring his name and telling him that she was very cold.

"Well, you just snuggle up to me, darlin'," he whispered back to the young beauty, his voice husky now, roughened by the surge of desire that had broken inside him like a wave breaking over the rocks of the far-off Monterey Peninsula.

As he drew the young woman still closer to him, Davy Watson caught the scent of her hair. Its fragrance intoxicated the Kansan, purging all thoughts of danger from his mind, and replacing them with perfumed imaginings and visions of desire. He leaned forward in the saddle and pressed his lips to the side of his lovely companion's neck.

She trembled and gasped, and called him her darling in a voice that shook with passion. Then she leaned back, turning her head and offering her full lips to the Kansan. And a moment later, as the stallion made its way up through the pines, their lips met in a long and hungry kiss.

Davy emitted a moan as his darting tongue entered the young beauty's mouth. A bonfire flared in the pit of his groin, and his cock grew as hot and stiff as the barrels of a Gatling gun that had just fired off a hundred rounds.

She gasped again as he caressed her breasts, and called out to God in a voice thick with desire. Then, as she pressed herself against him, squirming as she encountered the imperious stiffness of his erect sex, the young woman in Davy Watson's arms moaned like a timber wolf.

The Kansan turned his lovely young passenger around in the saddle, held her with his left hand, and began to undress her with his right. Then he unbuckled his belt and unbuttoned his pants, after which he grasped the young woman by her mid-section. His big hands nearly encircling her trim waist, Davy Watson first lifted her up, and then began to lower the young beauty onto his rigid and burning member. He entered her sopping, musky pussy, and the sudden access of heat and snugness took his breath away.

She called out to the deity once more. The barrel of her vagina gripped the Kansan snugly as she slid down the length of his pole, registering frequent and intense contractions every inch of the way. And when he clutched her firm buttocks and began to move her up and down, in gliding runs along the length of a cock whose moistened shaft now gleamed in the moonlight, the young woman's dark hair lashed from side to side as she shook her head to the cadence of her mounting passion and she cried out into the night, expressing her delight in disconnected phrases.

Up and down Davy Watson stroked, faster and faster, while his stallion continued on its wild course up through the mountain pines, its motion becoming the motion of the lovers. Up and down he stroked, guiding her snug, sweet pussy over his throbbing rod, generating a heat in his midsection which the Kansan imagined capable of igniting the leather of his saddle, sending it up in flames, to flare in the blackness like a torch at a tent meeting.

"Ooooh," Davy murmured, his eyes rolling up in his head as he felt a geyser about to erupt in the pit of his groin. The young beauty moaned back at him and rubbed herself against the Kansan, her sopping, clutching sex plastered against his groin, her straight, jet-black thatch mingling with his dark blond curls.

His pelvis began to jerk as he came, pumping volleys of jism into her.

She, in her turn, bucked wildly, dug her fingers into his hair, threw back her head and gasped as if she were expiring. And when she was finally still, the orgasmic convulsions having subsided, her mouth hung open and her eyes were shut; and her lips, the Kansan discovered, went suddenly cold, as cold as if she had been sucking on a piece of ice. The young woman sighed, shuddered reflexively, and then collapsed in his arms.

A few minutes later, the stallion reached level ground, and Davy Watson tightened his grip on the reins and slowed his mount to a walk. The big horse was breathing heavily, and it blew gusts of air through its nostrils, sending thick jets of vapor out into the chill night.

Still sighing and shuddering, still fused together at the groin, their handsome young bodies silvered by the moonlight, the lovers sat together in the saddle. The stallion snorted and whinnied twice as the Kansan pulled on the reins and drew it to a halt. After long moments spend in nuzzling, caressing, and kissing, the lovers parted, dressed, and dismounted by the shore of a broad mountain lake. There they refreshed themselves, and then the Kansan tended to his lathered stallion.

For over an hour they sat by the edge of the mountain lake, cradled in each other's arms. A rustling in the bushes at the far end of the clearing in which they sat finally interrupted their embrace. Davy gestured for silence. He eased his big Walker Colt out of its holster as he rose to his feet. Then, as he made his way to the far end of the clearing, the Kansan stopped for an instant to turn and gaze at the dark-eyed young beauty who sat waiting for him by the water's edge.

Moving ahead once more, the Kansan held his Colt lightly and wore a smile on his face, for he was sure that the newcomer was none other than his Pawnee blood-brother, who had decoyed his pursuers and arranged to meet Davy by the mountain lake.

He made out a shadowy figure in the moonlight, just emerging from a clump of pines. . . . His blood ran cold when he saw that it was not Soaring Hawk.

The man's gun was coming out of its holster, and as the Kansan leveled his own weapon, he saw the barrel of the intruder's gun gleam in the moonlight. Emitting a grunt of surprise, Davy Watson tightened his finger on the trigger of the Colt.

Blam! Bam! Blam! Bambam!

Guns roared and a series of brief, bright flashes lit the far end of the clearing. Raquel Mirabal screamed as she rose to her feet. Both men fell to the ground. As Raquel reached the scene of the gunplay, she gasped when she saw the bloody wound on the left side of the Kansan's head.

Davy Watson's eyes rolled up in their sockets, and he gave out with a long, plaintive sigh as he rolled down over a big rock. The Walker Colt dropped from his hand, and the Kansan pitched backward off the rock, disappearing with a loud splash into the dark icy waters of the lake.

At the same time that the Kansan disappeared beneath the surface of the water, Bart Braden lurched dizzily to his feet. Clutching the bloody wound in his left shoulder, the Texas ramrod advanced upon a horrified Raquel Mirabal.

"I come fer ya, honey," the big Texan told Don Solomon Mirabal's daughter, smiling like a wolf catching sight of a solitary lamb.

1

The Man Who Shot Davy Watson

The man who shot Davy Watson and then carried off Raquel Mirabal, as she lay in a dead faint beside the body of the young man who had been her very first lover only an hour before, rode south out of Lincoln County, and away from the bloody range war he had precipitated in order that he might possess the beautiful *chicana*, heading back to the relative safety and security of Texas, his home state.

Bart Braden had what he came for, and he had gotten it by gambling everything on one reckless throw of the dice, by rolling a natural seven which cleared the board and gave the Texas ramrod his heart's desire. The stakes in the New Mexican adventure had been very high, and the other players in the deadly game were not so fortunate as he.

Don Solomon Mirabal, Raquel's father, and the most powerful *patrón* among the New Mexico sheepmen, had lost his favorite child, and the lives of many of his devoted *partidarios*, as a consequence of the range war which had been sparked by the invasion of the hated *tejanos*, the hereditary enemies of the New Mexicans.

Bill Fanshaw had lost big, too. The cattle baron,

whose empire rivalled those of John Chisum and Charlie Goodnight, had been hoodwinked by Bart Braden into invading the pasturelands of Don Solomon Mirabal when the ramrod had deceived him by witholding word of a proposed settlement with the sheepmen of the New Mexico Territory.

In order to get the jump on his rivals, the Texas cattle baron had sent Braden, his foreman and ramrod, to negotiate the purchase of a strip of grazing land at the edge of the don's territory. This move would have then enabled Fanshaw to drive his Longhorn herds due north, and reach the rail-heads there long before any of his competitors.

At first the outraged New Mexicans bridled at this, at the thought of giving the hated *tejano* enemy a foothold in the pasturelands which their fathers had fought and died to possess. But compromise eventually prevailed. Profit was the god of the *tejanos*, the sheepmen reasoned, and this singular concession would make Bill Fanshaw their loyal ally, and thus pit his interests against those of his fellow cattle barons. The first loyalty of Fanshaw and his fellow Texans was to the *Yanqui* greenback, and not to each other.

Instead of the luxurious strip the cattle baron had originally requested, the sheepmen offered him one far to the west. . .where the Texans would have to contend with the mountains on one side and the Apaches on the other.

This compromise would be no great loss to the sheepmen, and it shifted to the Texans the problem of dealing with the fierce and marauding Jicarilla and Mimbreño Apache bands. Instead of being truly a concession, this sage move would actually

12

strengthen the dons' control of their lands, which were in constant danger of *tejano* encroachment from the south. Bill Fanshaw, from his southern headquarters in the new settlement of Roswell, would guarantee the security of his new allies' southernmost borders; the other Texan cattle barons were not likely to risk a direct confrontation with a man who had no peers but the giants of the southwestern cattle industry.

Knowing that Fanshaw would still agree to this modification of his offer, preferring such a concession to riskier long-range objectives which might well only be obtained at the cost of a bloody and protracted range war, the New Mexican *ricos* sent as their emissary to the cattle baron none other than Davy Watson. The Kansan and Soaring Hawk, his Pawnee blood-brother, had earlier rescued some sheepherders from lynching by a number of rampaging Texans, and were currently enjoying the gratitude and hospitality of Don Solomon Mirabal.

It was during this time that the Kansan had met the eighteen-year-old Raquel, the don's youngest daughter, a hot-blooded but virginal young beauty on the threshold of womanhood. And Bart Braden had been there, too, having come during the fiesta of *La Conquistadora* to deliver the cattle baron's offer.

It was at that time the Texas ramrod became infatuated with the dark and lovely *chicana*. But Raquel Mirabal's attentions were focussed in the direction of the Kansan, whose square-jawed, blond and blue-eyed good looks, and tales of his perilous and colorful escapades had totally captivated her. But Bart Braden was not in the least dissuaded by the turn of events; he was a man in the grip of an obsession, and had vowed not to rest until the don's young daughter was his.

And possess her he did—at a cost that littered the pasturelands and ajoining *Llano Estacado* with the bodies of men and animals, sheep and cattle, Indians, *chicanos* and whites. Bart Braden had summoned the Angel of Death to New Mexico, and that dark figure swept in on horseback, armed with a Winchester rifle and a Colt revolver.

The New Mexicans had dispatched a *gringo* to deal with *gringos*—but he was one whom they had learned to trust; and if Davy Watson and his companions had only reached Bill Fanshaw, the Angel of Death would not have scoured the New Mexican lands. But the Kansan was intercepted by Braden, who, once he had learned of Davy's mission, clubbed the Kansan unconscious with his gunbutt, took him prisoner, and kept him hidden from Bill Fanshaw.

The cattle baron, deceived by his ramrod into believing that his offer had been rejected out-of-hand, had then led his men on a sweep into the lands of Don Solomon Mirabal. He was determined to force a showdown with the *patrón*, and take as his booty a generous piece of the man's easternmost grazing lands, which would then give him uncontested access to the railheads to the north, thus enabling Fanshaw to market his cattle weeks ahead of his rivals' herds in the eager and clamoring markets of the East.

Bart Braden had come across Davy Watson and his three companions—Soaring Hawk and two of the sons of Don Solomon Mirabal—as they were being subjected to an ordeal by fire in the camp of Pahanca, a Comanche chief. The Comanches had recently run off a great number of Fanshaw cattle, and had traded them off to a pair of *Comancheros*, with whom the Kansan and his companions had unwittingly been traveling.

In the middle of the night, Davy and his friends found themselves encircled by a band of ferocious Comanches. The *Comancheros* then dispensed liquor and firearms to the Indian rustlers, taking the Texas cattle in return and riding off toward the Arizona border. The Kansan and his friends were thus abruptly abandoned by their erstwhile traveling companions and left to the tender mercies of the whooping and screaming Comanches, who became drunker and more savage with every passing minute.

Only a surprise attack by the Texans saved Davy and his companions from being burnt alive in the bonfire around which the wild, drunken Comanches danced. The Texans, having no sympathy for cattle rustlers of any stripe, slaughtered the Indians to a man. After that, having found out about Davy's mission, Braden knocked the Kansan unconscious and ordered him taken back to Fanshaw's headquarters in Roswell—away from the cattle baron, who was at that very moment riding north at the head of a band of armed men to join his ramrod.

Bart Braden had unleashed the whirlwind, and the Texan gave little thought to the consequences of his reckless act. His only concern was with the taking of Raquel Mirabal. And so, armed to the teeth and spoiling for a fight, the Texans thundered off, heading for the great *hacienda* of Don Solomon Mirabal.

Sweeping all before them, Fanshaw's riders traveled over the don's lands with all the fury of a windswept prairie fire. The sheepmen had been caught unawares, and before long the *tejano* enemy had the don's *hacienda* itself under siege.

Under normal conditions the sheepmen could have held out indefinitely. But a new factor had been introduced into the deadly equation: Braden had brought with him a Conestoga wagon filled with dynamite, the new explosive perfected only a few years before by the Swedish chemist Alfred Nobel.

Vowing to destroying the *hacienda* piecemeal, Braden had demonstrated the awesome power of the new explosive and given Don Solomon a last chance to capitulate.

Not while he lived, the stubborn old New Mexican patriarch told the Texans. *On your head be it*, was the judgment of Bill Fanshaw. *But at least evacuate your women and children from the hacienda*, he told the don, not wishing to answer for the blood of innocents.

Mirabal agreed to this, and in a matter of moments the women and children filed out of the embattled building. Here Bart Braden saw his chance, and had Raquel Mirabal sequestered and put under the watchful eye of one of his most trusted hands. The ramrod then returned to Fanshaw's side, where he had been conducting the siege.

The cattle baron knew nothing of his foreman's

16

machinations, and had been shaken to the core by the revelation of the new explosive's incredible power and destructive potential. It was with a heavy heart that he gave Braden permission to resume the storming of the Mirabal *hacienda*.

Great sections of the *hacienda's* stucco walls were blown away, and its red brick roof tiles were sent high into the air, reduced to smithereens as they shot out of sight. And moments later, when the echoes of the earthquake-roar that was the dynamite blast had subsided, the plaza in front of the Mirabal *hacienda* was filled with a ghastly pattering, the thudding sounds of the explosion's debris coming to earth in a bloodchilling rain.

"Give up, Don Solomon!" Bill Fanshaw cried hoarsely, *"For you have no other chance to remain alive!"*

"Even though I die, my family's honor remains alive!" was the essence of what the proud *hidalgo* shot back at the cattle baron.

"There's nothin' fer it but to blow the old fool to Kingdom Come," Fanshaw said with a sad expression and a shake of his leonine head, as he gave Bart Braden permission to resume the siege.

The end was almost at hand, and with it would come the fruition of the ramrod's plans. Once the *hacienda* had been blown apart and the hand-to-hand fighting had begun, he would take Raquel Mirabal and ride off with her, turning his back forever upon his fellow Texans and Bill Fanshaw, the one man whom he had always respected.

That was what Bart Braden had intended to do, but Fortune, which up to that time had been in league with the ramrod, was to have it otherwise.

17

A series of explosions suddenly wrought havoc in the ranks of the Texans, causing great dismay and disorder among them, as well as eliciting cheers from the desperate defenders of the Mirabal *hacienda*. About to depart with Raquel, the ramrod was forced to leave her and hasten to rally the Texans.

The confusion had been caused by none other than Davy Watson and his three companions, who had managed to escape from Roswell and streak northward in hopes of aiding the New Mexicans and saving Raquel Mirabal from Bart Braden. Davy had learned of this from Bill Fanshaw's daughter, who set him free to punish Bart Braden.

Wreaking havoc among the Texans, the Kansan and his Pawnee blood-brother were able to rescue Raquel Mirabal and ride off with her before the invaders had regained the upper hand in the battle.

The cowboys suddenly found themselves leaderless as they came up the dynamited corpse of Bill Fanshaw, and word soon spread that Bart Braden lay buried beneath a fallen wall. And indeed, the ramrod was nowhere to be seen. A short time after that, they were driven from the *hacienda* and sent in full flight back to Roswell, as reinforcements reached the Mirabal spread.

Davy and Soaring Hawk had streaked off into the night, to the foothills in the west. Three Texans streaked after them in hot pursuit, and were decoyed by the wily Pawnee.

Alone with the Latin beauty for the first time, the Kansan made love to her on horseback, after the fashion of the Huns, Cossacks and Comanches. They dismounted to rest by a lake in the high pines,

Raquel Mirabal gazing at the handsome young man beside her with wide, adoring eyes.

Later that night, Davy heard a crackling in the underbrush and went to investigate, certain that it was Soaring Hawk, who was to meet him at the mountain lake. But it was not the Pawnee whom he encountered.

The men fired simultaneously, and both took a bullet. Raquel Mirabal screamed as the Kansan's body rolled down the slope before her and disappeared into the dark, chill waters of the lake. Smiling as he clutched his wounded shoulder, Bart Braden came after Raquel Mirabal.

Davy Watson had luck on his side, and when Soaring Hawk had doubled back to the mountain lake, having eluded his pursuers, the Pawnee brave found the Kansan clinging to some bushes by the edge of the water.

Braden's bullet had creased the side of Davy's skull, and its impact had caused him to lose consciousness. In the darkness of the copse of pines where the sudden shootout had occurred, the Texas ramrod, taking Davy Watson's bullet at the same time that he gunned down the Kansan, left his enemy for dead as he watched the latter's body roll down the grassy slope and pitch into the still, icy waters of the lake.

Soaring Hawk pulled his blood-brother out of the water and tended to him. Apart from a wound that would heal to a livid scar at his hairline, over his left temple, and a headache that he would wake up with for the next week, Davy Watson was unharmed. But his pride had been hurt, and the Kansan vowed not to rest until he had avenged himself upon Bart Braden and rescued Raquel Mirabal.

"Guess we'll jus' take us a l'il ride down Texas-way," he muttered darkly, staring toward the south with flinty eyes and a hard, cold smile.

His face a stoic mask, Soaring Hawk nodded at this. The Pawnee greatly desired to return to his people, as they hunted the ever-dwindling buffalo herds on the prairies of western Kansas and eastern Colorado, but he was by now resigned to the quirks of fate which had so far prevented the two men from returning to their homes and loved ones. The Plains Indian acknowledged the power of destiny in men's affairs, and was duly resigned to the frequent interruptions along the trail that led back to home.

Despite the fact that Bart Braden did not expect anyone to be coming after him so soon, least of all the man he had left for dead, and despite the fact that the Texan's trail was still warm, Davy Watson was not ready to streak off in hot pursuit of Raquel Mirabal's abductor.

The Kansan felt that it was necessary to return to the Mirabal *hacienda*, and inform Raquel's father of what had transpired. Don Solomon had been his host, and Davy felt compelled to reward the sheep-man's kindness and generosity by explaining to the *patrón* that his favorite daughter was alive and well, despite having fallen prey to Bart Braden, the *tejano* enemy.

Upon their return to the Mirabal spread, the blood-brothers saw to their relief that the siege had been lifted, and that the invading Texans, rendered leaderless by the death of Bill Fanshaw and the defection of the obsessed Bart Braden, had been sent flying back to the south in defeat.

Davy was not worried about losing Braden's trail because the circumstance of an *Anglo* and a *Chicana* traveling alone in Texas was rare in the extreme. As long as Braden kept Raquel with him, the tracking of the ramrod would present no great problem for the trail-savvy Kansan and his Pawnee blood-brother.

Upon hearing of Raquel's abduction, the New Mexicans were furious. They volunteered—almost to a man—to ride after Bart Braden. But no, the don told them as he shook his head, a sad and tired smile upon his lips, this was not possible. People of Mexican blood were regarded as second-class citizens in the state of Texas, and a large band of heavily armed Mexican-Americans thundering across the border would be regarded as tantamount to an act of war. The Texans had long memories, and they still harbored hard feelings regarding their treatment in the days prior to the Mexican War. Any force of *chicanos* entering the Lone Star state would cause the *tejanos* to rise up in strength and annihilate it. No, the rescue of Raquel Mirabal by her own people was, for the present, at least, an impossibility.

When Davy Watson informed his listeners that he and Soaring Hawk were off after Bart Braden, the New Mexicans heaved a collective sigh of relief. Don Solomon and his three sons held a high opinion of the valor of the Kansan and *El Indio* (as they called Soaring Hawk), and were profuse in the expression of their gratitude.

The next morning, having thoroughly rested their horses and been generously provisioned, Davy Watson and Soaring Hawk rode off as the dawn began to tinge the eastern sky of the New Mexico Territory with its first, tentative washes of purple, violet and pink. The two men rode off to the south, where the dark sky had only begun to lighten, toward the wild and sprawling land known as the state of Texas.

In 1870, the geography of Western Texas was divided into two sections—the settled territory between the Colorado and the Nueces, and the open, barren wastes that bordered the Rio Grande.

The fertile area, whose flat coastal prairies extended inland for some forty miles, began to rise in gentle swells at that point, running on to the foothills of the Guadalupe range, 150 miles from the Gulf of Mexico.

Rich and broad pastures, characterized by thick, waving grasses, were the predominant feature of this terrain, noted for its abundant grazing in both winter and summer. This was the Texas cattle country; the land that first nurtured the herds which had provided a large portion of the nation's supply of beef after the Civil War.

Advancing westward across the state, the soil grew steadily in fertility, being lavishly distributed in this part of Texas as a black calcareous loam. And where the streams in the other parts of the Lone Star State tended to flow thick and muddy, the waters in Western Texas were as clear as the eye of a sober and upright man. The land was, as many visitors had remarked, as beautiful and luxuriant as any region in the world, bar none.

There were drawbacks, however, which held West Texas back and caused it to fall somewhat short of being a veritable paradise on earth. A relative scarcity of timber inhibited building and fencing, while the dry seasons wrought havoc with the abundant crops; and Indian raids upon the frontier still made settlement in that area a somewhat risky business. In addition to this, counterbalancing the abundant and near-constant summer breeze from the gulf were the northers—furious winter winds that shot down from the upland plains, capable of ravaging great stretches of land in a very short time.

Another problem was that of the Mexicans in the region, of whom there were between twenty and thirty thousand. Relations between the "greasers" and the *gringos* had rarely been amicable, and many Texans of both stripes remembered the vicious fighting prior to and during the Mexican War. The wounds of those years of conflict were far from healed.

The Texans were notorious for their prejudice against non-whites in general, and Mexicans in particular. After the war, those Mexicans who had property and wealth withdrew to Old Mexico, leaving their less fortunate fellows to the mercies of the hated *tejanos*.

They were regarded by the Texans as only a step above Negroes on the social ladder, and were used largely as a supply of cheap labor in the areas of argriculture and stock-raising. Even though, in theory, the Mexican-Americans were considered citizens of Texas, with suffrage equal to that of the whites, in reality they were largely denied access to the state's political machinery.

Another group to figure largely in the way of life of the region were the German immigrants, of whom there were between thirty and forty thousand at the time. In several counties, such as Fayette, Caldwell and Travis, as well as the city of San Antonio, the Germans numbered about one-third of the total population. In Calhoun, Bastrop and Bexar (excluding the aforementioned San Antonio), they constituted one-half of the population. And in Comal, Gillespie and Medina counties, nearly all the inhabitants were German. This predominance had begun to wane as the seventies began, but at the time, the Germans were still a major influence in Western Texas.

German associations required the immigrants to come to these shores in possession of a certain amount of capital ($120 for single men and $240 for married men), thereby excluding a pauper class. The first waves consisted largely of peasants and mechanics, and those who had been able to escape German justice due to their emigration. The hardy, energetic and hard-working Germans adapted well to frontier conditions, and were soon acknowledged by the American residents of West Texas as their pioneering equals.

After the European revolutions of 1848, many farmers and persons of moderate means came to the New World, seeking a better future. Many cultivated men of liberal tendencies came to the American shores then, in hopes of creating a more tolerant society than the repressive and reactionary feudal Europe they had fled.

These new immigrants brought little capital with them and, following the German tendency to invest their money in land, were extremely limited in funds as they began their residence in the new country. But to offset this material lack, the new Germans brought with them rich and diverse intellectual lives and many refinements of taste: the *kultur* of Germany had taken root in the soil of western Texas.

The lifestyle of these new and liberal settlers was often bizarre and incongruous, as European refinement contrasted sharply with their rough backwoods life. As one American author had reported in 1860:

"You are welcomed by a figure in a blue flannel shirt and pendant beard, quoting Tacitus, having in one hand a long pipe, in the other a butcher's knife; Madonnas upon log-walls; coffee in tin cups upon Dresden saucers; barrels for seats, to hear a Beethoven's symphony on the grand piano; 'My wife made these pantaloons, and my stockings grew in the field yonder'; a fowling-piece that cost $300, and a saddle that cost $5; a book-case half-filled with classics, half with sweet potatoes.

"But, as lands are subdued, and capital is amassed, these inconveniences will disappear, and pass in amusing traditions, while the sterling education and high-toned character of the fathers will be unconsciously transmitted to the social benefit of the coming generation.

"The virtues I have ascribed to them as a class are not, however, without the relief of faults, the most prominent among which are a free-thinking and a devotion to reason, carried in their turn, to the verge of bigotry, and expanded to a certain rude licence of manners and habits, consonant with their wild prairies, but hardly with the fitness of things, and, what in practical matters is even worse error, an insane mutual jealousy, and petty bickering that prevents all prolonged and effective cooperation—an old German ail, which the Atlantic has not sufficed to cleanse.''

Germans, Mexicans, Indians pillaging the frontier, and the tetchy-proud, whang leather-tough Texans: such was the volatile human composition of the wild and open land through which Bart Braden rode, taking with him his captive, the dark-haired, sloe-eyed young daughter of the New Mexican *rico*, Don Solomon Mirabal.

Down from the lawless New Mexico Territory the Texas ramrod had ridden, the protesting Raquel Mirabal in tow, her wrists bound before her as she sat in her saddle; down through the Guadalupe Mountains, and into the Lone Star State, skirting its highest point, Guadalupe Peak, en route.

Riding east of the Delaware Mountains, Braden traversed Culberson County and headed south into the Jeff Davis mountain range. Thence eastward, along the course of the Pecos River, through cow-towns like Royalty and Barstow, through river-towns such as Grandfalls and Girvin.

Southward over the Stockton Plateau, and then to the east, over the great open expanse that is the

Edwards Plateau. Farther east, and then southeast, through Telegraph, Medina and Bandera, and into Bexar County, stopping at last in the city of San Antonio.

Riding along an old road that followed a creek bottom, dotted with houses which stood in the shade of live-oaks, trees extremely rare to these parts, Braden and Raquel Mirabal rode the last miles to San Antonio.

In the afternoon the two rode through the clean and quiet streets of one of the small German towns. Braden reined in the horses by the gate of a little cottage whose windows and shutters were edged with a white trim. From within the cottage there came the sounds of people singing. Several voices could be heard, both male and female, sustaining the German song's parts with sweet and well-trained voices.

"Damn, but that there's a purty air," Braden drawled softly, turning his face toward Raquel Mirabal, who sat beside him, her hands no longer bound.

For an instant the beautiful young *chicana's* expression softened, and she nodded slowly. Her eyes lowered, not meeting the bold and intense look of the Texan.

A slight smile came to Braden's lips, only to disappear an instant later. It was the first time that Raquel had responded to him with anything less than anger and contempt.

He sat unmoving in his saddle, staring at her, his strong features set in a mask of impassivity, which was in direct contrast to his searching and hungry eyes. Braden said nothing else as the music soared

27

to a crescendo, the male and female voices rising in heartbreakingly beautiful unison. Raquel's acknowledgement of his statement was enough for him. He regarded it as progress in his strange courtship of Don Solomon's daughter. He sat looking at her, and was content, having absolutely no desire to press his luck. It was progress enough.

At this time, coming up the quiet street, Braden saw a tame doe, wearing a band on its neck to identify it for hunters. It was delicate and graceful, and so tame that it passed within two feet of Raquel's horse. And when she gently leaned over and reached down her hand, the doe paused to lick it. A moment later the young deer left, just as the song was concluding.

"Mebbe we jus' might mosey back hereabouts, one of these days," Bart Braden said under his breath as he flicked his reins, taking one last look at Raquel Mirabal.

Her long black hair glowed softly in the late afternoon light, and her beautiful face reminded the Texan of a carved angel he had once seen in an old Spanish mission on the outskirts of the border town of Del Rio.

Away from the river, and onto the great plain at whose edge San Antonio lies, Braden and Raquel rode. To the west, gentle slopes descended toward the plain; and past that, looking north, the riders saw the gradual rise of land which led to the mountain country.

A thin edging of trees around the city's river provided the only relief on the broad, surrounding landscape of limitless grass and thorny bushes. Mesquite, that short, thin, prickly relative of the locust tree, dotted the prairie, one of the most familiar and ubiquitous elements in the geography of Western Texas. Often the mesquite mixed with other prickly shrubs, such as chapparal, and formed an impenetrable barrier to overland travel for great stretches of ground.

Coming over the western prairie, Braden and Raquel saw the city of San Antonio in the distance, its domes and clustered white houses gleaming gently in the first rays of the sunset. Both of them gazed with interest upon the city's picturesque jumble of buildings, its odd and antiquated foreign aspect.

It had a solemn, Latin air about it, one which contrasted strangely with the rattling life of the Anglos, whose commerce enlivened San Antonio's dusty streets. The streets themselves were crowded with strolling Mexicans, as well as a fair proportion of Germans and Texans.

The display of nationalities was most evident in the shape and style of San Antonio's houses. The American dwellings were set back from the street, and characterized by three-story brick structures, galleries and jalousies, and gardens whose picket fences bordered the walks of the houses.

Trimmer and less four-square were the houses of the Germans, rising gracefully above the old streets, their pink window-blinds contributing a vibrant touch of color to the scene.

All low, and made of adobe or stone, the Mexican dwellings were colored by a wash of either white or blue, and had their single story trimmed sharply by a flat roof.

The eastern entrance to the city had as its most

outstanding feature the square of the Alamo, that bloody landmark in the violent history of Texas. Windowless cabins of mud-daubed stakes, roofed with *tula*, the abundant river grass, were prominent in the area, as were houses of gray, unburnt adobe, whose rooves were better-thatched, and at whose doors there lounged groups of brown-skinned Mexicans.

Upon the far side of the San Antonio river lay the principal part of San Antonio. The river, never varying in height or temperature, flowed beneath the low bridge, sparkling with its limpid and crystalline beauty. It had a rich blue color, and flowed silently and swiftly over a bottom covered with pebbles, and between banks that grew thick with reeds. The bridge and the river combined there to form a place of great beauty and serenity.

The plaza was a strange and anachronous composite. Old and embattled walls, sturdy and Spanish, alternated with American hotels and glass-fronted stores; and from the dome of the stuccoed and forbidding old Spanish cathedral, the call to vespers rang out jaggedly from a cracked bronze bell whose jarring music expressed the plaza's dissonant theme of clashing cultures.

Not far outside the city, along the river, the old Spanish missions were to be found. Ponderous and overbearing, but possessing at the same time a rude grandeur, the missions were enduring monuments to the bravery and ardor of the Spanish *padres* who were among the first Europeans to penetrate the wild and savage country. Foremost among these missions in earliest times had been the Alamo, now a hacked and battered monument to Texan courage.

Aqueducts extended around the city for miles in all directions, revealing to the student of cultures that a larger population had existed when the place was under the Mexican flag. Many of these *acequias* came to be abandoned, but many were still in use, watering extensive garden patches when Bart Braden and Raquel Mirabal rode into San Antonio.

As they made their way into the heart of town, Braden noticed the plump and black-eyed young Mexican girls, conversing animatedly as they strolled the streets that led to the city's main plaza, followed by the erect and dignified figures of the dark and wrinkled matrons who served as their *duennas*.

Mexican men in large sombreros and gaily embroidered short jackets strolled around the plaza, or lounged against brick or adobe walls, smoking cigarillos, singing in Spanish to the music of guitars and laughing raucously from time to time.

Distinct from the Mexicans were the taller Texans, who strolled the plaza with long, loping strides, smoking cigarettes rolled from wheatstraw or chewing tobacco and letting fly great brown gobbets of tobacco juice.

Felt and ten-gallon hats were worn by the *tejanos,* with an occasional Stetson crowning the head of some of the more prosperous-looking citizens. Boot leather creaked and spurs jingled as the Texans exchanged salty observations in their slow drawls, slapping their pants or the leather holsters on their belts as they broke out into loud, sudden guffaws.

Also noticeable in the plaza were the bearded Germans, conspicuous by their starched collars, polished boots and neat suits. Erect and precise, they strolled around as if on a military tour of inspection, greeting one another with elaborate politeness, often doffing their bowlers, derbies and caps as they stopped to click their heels together and bow.

On the plaza, and on the streets leading into it, many of the older Mexican buildings had been remodeled and brought "up-to-date," and were now serving as drinking places, run after the example of New Orleans saloons, the signs on their gaudy fronts simply proclaiming "Exchange."

Outside these saloons and honkytonks the customers loitered, either roughly or exquisitely attired, their dress proclaiming the tone of the establishment before which they stood.

The presence of so many Mexican-Americans made Bart Braden edgy as he rode beside the young *chicana* whom he had abducted from her father's *hacienda*, and the ramrod's right hand was never far from the big Colt .45 that sat loosely in its weathered holster.

All it would take, he reckoned, was one appeal from Raquel Mirabal, one cry of anguish and alarm, followed by the declaration that the *gringo* at her side had recently stolen her away from her people in the New Mexico Territory.

As a number of the Mexicans whom they passed were wearing sidearms, there was a strong probability that Raquel's appeal would not go unheeded. But Raquel did not cry out. Biding her time, she waited for the chance to escape from the infatuated ramrod without being responsible for any further bloodshed, for the sight of the Kansan's shooting had made a deep impression upon the eighteen-year-old girl.

Another reason for her silence was that she had grudgingly begun to respect Bart Braden. The Texan had never forced himself upon her, always treating Raquel with the utmost respect and *cortesia*, almost as if he were a Mexican himself. And formidable as the agile, powerful cowboy was, he would not permit any man to behave toward her with less than total politeness and decorum.

Having recovered from the initial shock of her abduction, the strong-willed and resilient young daughter of Don Solomon Mirabal had determined to avenge herself upon Bart Braden. It would be necessary to lull him into a false sense of confidence first, so she had decided to bide her time. But the Texan would get what was coming to him, she vowed to herself, as sure as mesquite grows in West Texas.

Braden's horse drew to a halt in the street, facing a large and noisy emporium, outside of which were clustered a number of rough-looking types. Raquel's horse stopped beside the Texan's as Braden swung a leg over his saddle horn and leaped to the ground with a display of easy agility. He was beside Raquel's horse a moment later, and reached up to help her out of the saddle.

"Le's go inside, honey," he said softly as his big hands went around her trim waist. Saying nothing, Raquel Mirabal looked past the Texas ramrod as

33

he gently lowered her to the ground.

"By gum, if it ain't ol' Bart Braden, hisself!" a gruff voice called out from behind Braden, just as the latter had put the young *chicana* down. Quick as lightning, the ramrod spun around, his hand poised over his holstered Colt.

A huge bearded man, with eyes as beady and mean as those of a polecat, smiled at Braden, revealing a mouthful of snaggle teeth whose appearance and spacing brought to mind a weathered picket fence. He wore a dusty old slouch hat, a heavy jacket of the type associated with stagecoach drivers and muleskinners, baggy woolen trousers, and thick, low-heeled miners boots which were caked with a heavy coating of mud.

"By God, Bart, don't hoist that piece up at me," the man went on, still smiling his gap-toothed smile, his hot, glittering little eyes now traveling over Raquel Mirabal's shapely form. "It's me, Ford Sweinhardt. Don't you remember me, Bart?" the big bearded man asked in an oily, wheedling voice. "I was with ya when you done rid herd on Jasper Lyons' Longhorns, up Pecos way."

Braden's eyes narrowed as he stared at the man.

" 'Member the time we done rid down into Mexico to git ol' Jasper's cattle back? Well, I'll say we 'bout kicked us some ass that day—'member, Bart? Done tore up them greasers, brought back the herd, an' more'n a hundred Spanish-speakin' cows to boot! 'Twas the next best thing to the Mexican War."

For an instant, Braden's eyes darted nervously over to Raquel Mirabal, who was at his side, taking in the spectacle of the big, bearded man, as were all the men around him. Then, as the ramrod's eyes lit on the speaker once more, a razor's edge smile came to his thin lips.

" 'Member now, Bart?" the man asked eagerly, his gruff voice squeaking as it rose to a higher register.

Braden nodded slowly, his eyes now colder than a norther, the cold sudden wind which sweeps across the upland prairies to the north in the winter months.

"Yeah, I remember you, Sweinhardt," the ramrod said in a voice that expressed absolutely no emotion.

"What brings ya here'bouts, Bart?" the man persisted, not in the least discouraged by Braden's unenthusiastic greeting.

"I come to see Ollie Entwhistle," the ramrod muttered, holding out his arm for Raquel Mirabal to take.

"Well, he's still goin' strong. You can bet yer boots on that. Still serves the biggest steak an' the baddest whiskey in West Texas."

Braden nodded as he and Raquel began to make their way through the crowd of rough men, all of whom cast long and lingering looks at the lovely young *chicana*, once she had walked past them.

"It's real good to see you agin, Bart," the big bearded man said unctuously.

Braden did not respond to this. He thrust open the swinging door before him and nodded to Raquel, his smile softening as he met her eyes.

Music issued from within the honkytonk, along with the sour reek of stale beer and the sharp smell

of spilled whiskey on sawdust. A battered old upright piano, stirdent and jangling as its hammers
beat out an off-key tune with relentless authority,
cut through the babel of the crowd with the
violence of a rusty cleaver smashing through beef
bones.

"*O, way down yonder in the land of cotton,*"
the piano player sang in a raw baritone voice that
suitably complemented his instrument, "*old times
there are not forgotten. Look away, look away,
look a-wa-aaay, Dixieland.*"

A chorus of Rebel yells rose throughout the bar,
as a number of former Confederates lifted high
their glasses in drunken and sentimental tribute to
the Old South, whose memory was still cherished in
many parts of the American Southwest.

"Who was that *hombre*?" someone asked
outside, after Bart Braden had escorted Raquel
Mirabal into Oliver Entwhistle's honkytonk.

"Got the look of a man what means business,
I'll say that for him," a man with a high-pitched
voice called.

"Oh, that he does," the big bearded man named
Sweinhardt growled. "Hardest man I ever did see.
Don't fear nothin' that walks, flies or swims. An'
he'd draw on the devil hisself, if'n he had a mind
to." He nodded and smiled a wry, admiring smile.
"Ol' Bart Braden's quick as a panther an' hard as
Pittsburgh steel. An' the best damn ramrod an'
foreman anybody ever done seen."

" 'Zat so?" remarked a fat, balding man in a
checkered flannel shirt, who stood beside
Sweinhardt.

"You ain't jus' whistlin' *Dixie*, boy," Sweinhardt told the man. "I done worked with him, up Pecos way, fer over two year." He shook his head. "Most unstoppable sum' bitch I ever did see. Ain't nobody yet ever got on his bad side an' lived to tell about it."

"Who's the l'il *tamale* he brung with him?" someone else asked.

"Dunno," grunted Sweinhardt. "But she's a hot-lookin' piece, ain't she?"

"I'll say she is, bedad!" piped an old man with a stubbly white beard.

"That's the one good thing you can say fer them greasers," Sweinhardt told the men gathered around him, nodding solemnly as he did. "They sure got 'em a passel of fine-lookin' women. I will say that fer 'em."

"Then why's the men so damn ugly?" someone called out in a whiskey tenor.

"All foreigners is ugly," Sweinhardt replied, settling the matter. "Leastwise, the menfolks is."

"Where's Ollie Entwhistle?" Bart Braden called out to the nearest of the four bartenders who worked the long bar that occupied almost the entire left wall of the rectangular room.

"Back in his office, Bart," the man replied, breaking into a smile as he recognized the ramrod.

Braden nodded. "Thanks, Kingston," he said. "Donald McKillop still workin' here?"

The bartender shook his head as he wiped his hands on his stained apron. "Nope. Had hisself a li'l disagreement with ol' Charlie Shuttinger. Charlie pulled a knife on him once't—right here at the bar, an' ol' Donald winged him with that teensie l'il Smith an' Wesson .22 he allus wore

37

tucked in his vest."

Braden smiled at this. "I told him he couldn't bring down nothin' bigger'n a Rio Grande mosquito with that ol' pop-gun," he drawled.

"Well, he pegged Charlie in the arm," the bartender went on. "An' it was enough to make him drop the knife. Then Donald broke a bottle of Old Overholt across't his head, an' slung him out into the street. Dumped him smack in the middle of a big mud puddle."

Braden was grinning, now. "Hell, that ain't no big deal," he told the bartender. "That kinda thing happens in this place all the time."

"Well, that's true enough," the barkeep agreed. "But the onliest thing different there was that Shuttinger was married to the sister of Sheriff Roy Brubaker. An' ol' Roy, he didn't take too kindly to havin' his brother-in-law made a laughin'-stock of in his own bailiwick." The man paused to pick his nose.

"So ol' Roy comes in the next night, bellies up to the bar, orders him a double shot of red-eye; smiles real sweet-like at ol' Donald. . .an' tells him that if'n he's still in San Antone when the sun comes up in the mornin' he's a-gonna tar'n feather him, an' have him rid outta town on a rail."

"Trouble with Roy," Braden drawled, "he ain't got no sense of humor."

"*Humpf*," the bartender growled, taken aback by this thought. "Ain't nobody never cared to find out whether ol' Roy could take a joke or not."

"I did, once't," the ramrod said softly. "Back a few years. He was 'bout to run some tinhorn gambler out of town—when the gent was right in the middle of a big high-stakes poker game with me.''

The bartender's eyes widened. "You tell ol' Roy to wait?" he asked in a low voice.

Braden smiled. "I told ol' Roy that I done had a passel of money invested in that there gentleman, an' wouldn't he be so good as to wait until I had finished conductin' my business."

The bartender cleared his throat. "You said *that* to Roy?" he asked incredulously. "That man's one mean sum' bitch."

"That's as may be," Bart Braden said softly. "Ol' Roy, he got all red in the face, an' tol' the tinhorn that he better tighten his spats, an' dust off his Stetson, 'cause he was leavin' on the next stage out."

"Lord A'mighty," the bartender croaked. "Then what happened?"

"I told Roy I didn't think that was such a good idee," Braden drawled. "Then I told him to hang loose a li'l bit, whilst I finished conductin' my business with the tinhorn."

The bartender looked around nervously before speaking. "Ol' Roy, he prob'ly didn't take too kindly to your tellin' him that, now did he?"

There was a wry smile on the ramrod's face. "No, I reckon he didn't. When I told him that, he got all red in the face an' began to snort like a Mexican bull. 'An' what if I don't choose to hang loose?' he says to me, a-squintin' as if he was seein' me on the far end of a gunsight."

"Hoo-wee damn!" exclaimed the bartender. "What did ya do then, Bart?"

"Oh, I jus' smiled at ol' Roy, real friendly-like,"

the ramrod told him. "An' said that if'n he didn't let me conduct my business with the man, it was a good bet that San Antone was a-gonna have to get itself a new sheriff."

"What'd he do then?"

"He made a face like a Comanche who done lost his last horse, pulled out his gold watch, snapped open the lid, squinted at it fer a long time, an' then snapped it shut."

The bartender handed Braden a double shot of rye whiskey.

" 'You got four hours,' " the ramrod went on, "ol' Roy says without lookin' at me. An' then, he turns on his heel an' stomps out of the place."

"*You tol' him that San Antone'd need a new sheriff*?" the bartender asked in awe.

"Yep," Braden replied, smiling his tight, grim smile. "An' Roy's a good ol' boy. He done seen the humor in that."

"I'll say he did," the bartender chuckled. "What's the lady drinkin', Bart?" he asked.

Suddenly, Raquel stepped forward and leaned over the bar, facing the bartender.

"I have been abducted by this man," she told the barkeep, reinforcing her appeal by looking him right in the eye. "This man caused a range war in New Mexico, and took me away by force from my father's *hacienda*."

In response to this, the barkeep grinned sheepishly. "Shucks, I don' know nothin' 'bout that, miss," he mumbled, looking down at his shoes. "But ol' Bart, he's all right with me. 'Scuse me, but I got folks to serve," he said, turning and making his way down the bar.

"What do I owe ya, Jim?" a grinning Braden called out, while Raquel stared open-mouthed at the retreating bartender's back.

"Nothin' a-tall, Bart," the man called back over his shoulder. "That there's on the house. It's good to have ya back."

Stunned by the barkeep's response, Raquel Mirabal heaved a forlorn sigh. She was in Bart Braden's land now, she realized, and could expect no help from the *tejanos*, the hereditary enemies of her people.

The full moon sat high in the night sky of Texas, and its beams flooded through the window of a room in the city of San Antonio, edging the big bed, the night table beside it, and the polished boards at the foot of the bed with a cold, silver light.

In the darkest corner of the room a kerosene lamp cast its warmer light with an occasional flicker. Warm and cool, the two illuminations overlapped the center of the room, highlighting the bodies of the naked couple there with a strange and ghostly light.

This light seemed to shift and dance with a rippling brilliance on the broad muscular back of the man in the bed. It shone with the glint of burnished copper as it played over the long, fine hairs on his forearms, glinting again in that fashion as it highlighted his curly brown hair and long, thick sideburns.

Facing the man, lying on her back in the bed, the woman's dark eyes caught the light as she stared up

41

and smiled fiercely between gleaming, clenched teeth. Points of light glimmered in her thick black hair as well, as it fanned out beneath her head and shoulders, shining with the cold and far-off glimmer of distant stars.

Her back arched as she squirmed beneath his touch, and her firm, round breasts jutted up into the air, their thick, dark nipples erect and tender, pointing into the darkness like twin signposts of desire and arousal.

Sweat ran down in rivulets from the hollows of her arms, making irregular traceries as they traveled over her ribcage, the light glimmering on them with the semaphoric radiance of diamonds on a river bed.

The man's hand stroked the inside of the young woman's thigh, the nails of his fingers lightly raking the tender flesh there, causing it to rise in goose bumps. Further and further over her thigh his hand travelled, in a slow, upward course, heading toward the black, fleecy muff and pouting lips above.

"*Ay, ay, ay,*" the young *chicana* moaned as the man's middle finger suddenly parted those engorged nether lips and lightly worked its way up between them. And when he withdrew his finger, having completed his run, he caught the sharp, musky scent of her arousal.

"*Ay, Dios,*" she murmured, her thighs twitching and her pelvis jerking reflexively.

The man leaned over and began to nuzzle her neck, at the same time bringing his hand up to stroke and cup her breast. Then he lowered his head and began to run his tongue in light, flicking movements over her dark areola and nipple.

She sighed like the wind that soughs through the grasses of the *Llano Estacado*, and her body stiffened for an instant, before she broke out into a "Come inside me now, Bart."

Slowly, gently, the man's big hand traveled down over the young woman's body, stroking the quivering flesh beneath its fingers with infinite tenderness and great delicacy. And then, having descended over the gentle slope of her belly, the man's thick fingers entered the matted black tangle of the young *chicana's* pubic hair.

At the same time that his fingers descended, the man's mouth traveled in an upward course, grazing breasts and neck until his lips met and covered hers. The kiss was long and passionate, and the woman began to squirm as his finger stopped its stroking motion and suddenly penetrated her.

She responded with a short, sharp intake of breath, and a twitch of her pelvis. Slowly the man began to work his finger in and out of her sheath, his broad palm making contact with the fleshy cupola that was her mound of Venus.

"Oh, come inside me, *querido*," she whispered intensely, looking up at him with dark and gleaming eyes. "Come inside me now, Bart."

"Oh, honey," Bart Braden groaned as he felt the woman's long, tapering fingers encircle his hot and throbbing rod. Lightly, but firmly, she stroked him, running her hand back and forth over the length of his shaft.

"I want you, Bart," she whispered in that voice of rising wind, sighing with a passion as elemental as the currents that swept over the prairie.

Bart Braden groaned again as he withdrew his finger and raised himself up on his hands and knees, about to move toward her.

"Oh, Bart," the young *chicana* moaned, shifting beneath him and opening her legs as she prepared to take him inside her, still holding his hard, erect sex in her hand.

His forearms came down on both sides of her head, and the Texas ramrod's shadow fell over her face, causing the highlights in her dark eyes to disappear.

Just then the light of the kerosene lamp began to flicker and dance, as the flame burnt down on a wick that was nearly dry. For an instant, Bart Braden's face was bathed in bright light, which revealed a look of intense desire upon his face. His eyes were wide, and glazed with longing, giving the ramrod the look of a man of both great desperation and determination.

His mouth was set in a tight smile and he breathed through his nose in great, rapid blasts. And when the young *chicana* inserted Braden's rod into her wet, musky sheath, the Texan's mouth opened and he caught his breath with a gasp.

He moved his body toward her, and heard a soft, squishing sound as his sex began to glide into her warm and welcoming sheath.

She made a sound deep in her throat and raised her pelvis to meet him. "*Querido*," she murmured huskily as Bart Braden began to penetrate her with long, slow strokes.

They hit a stride and held it for a while, the Texan's tantalizing strokes finally causing the *chicana* to thrust at him more rapidly, urging him

44

on to greater exertions.

"Oh, honey," Braden moaned, after he had intensified his strokes and deepened his penetration for some time. His eyes were shut, and his body began to tremble as the dark and lovely young woman squirmed and moaned beneath him.

"Oh, honey," he said once more, as a railroad flare seemed to ignite somewhere in the back of his brain.

"Ra-quel," he groaned as the crucible in the pit of his groin overflowed, and the molten issue of his passion surged forth out of his jerking body.

"Oh, Raquel!" the ramrod cried out in the night, his anguished voice ringing off the white-washed adobe walls of the bedroom.

Oblivious to the ramrod's cries, the young woman beneath him bucked and thrashed, the force of her own climax tearing incoherent, guttural sounds out of her throat. And when both were satiated, they lay spent and panting in the silver Texas moonlight, the kerosene lamp having gone out a few moment earlier.

After several minutes, Bart Braden got out of bed and put on his clothes. He smiled a tight, grim smile and nodded to the young woman in the bed.

"Goo' night, ho-nee," she whispered back, the traces of a Mexican accent coloring her words. And as the ramrod turned and began to walk toward the door, the dark-haired young woman glanced over at the crumpled wad of greenbacks which sat upon her night table.

A moment later Bart Braden stepped out into the night, the moon over San Antonio silvering his spurs and the handle of his big Colt, and began to walk back toward Oliver Entwhistle's establishment, to where Raquel Mirabal slept a troubled sleep in the locked room which adjoined his.

2

The Kansan Comes To Texas

"Dah-veed, amigo," Anibal Mirabal, Raquel's eldest
brother, said to the Kansan as the latter and
Soaring Hawk mounted their horses in front of the
Mirabal hacienda, deep in the New Mexico
Territory. *"Dah-veed,* when you catch up with this
hombre, Bart Braden, please treat him with all the
cortesia and consideration that my father,
brothers, and I would show the *tejano* gentleman."

"Oh, don't worry, 'bout that, Anibal," the
Kansan replied to the New Mexican's irony. "I owe
that sum'bitch a bullet," he said, not realizing that
he *had* shot Braden in the exchange of bullets by
the mountain lake, in whose aftermath the Texan
had taken Raquel Mirabal and left him for dead.

"I owe that sum'bitch a bullet right 'twixt the
eyes," the Kansan told Anibal Mirabal and his
brothers. "And I aim to see the debt paid in full."

"Señor Watson," Don Solomon Mirabal called
out in his deep, resonant voice as he stood in the
doorway of the *hacienda*. "Promise me that you
will exercise all caution in your efforts to get my
daughter back from Braden."

Davy looked down at the *patrón's* stern visage
and pleading eyes. "That'll be my first concern,

Don Solomon," he told the sheepman reassuringly. "I ain't 'bout to settle Bart Braden's hash while Raquel's still his captive. Ol' Soaring Hawk here—" he nodded in the direction of the young Pawnee brave who sat astride an Indian pony—"an' me intends to make sure Raquel is safe and sound before we start with Braden." The Kansan smiled grimly. "But once't we got her clear, then we're goin' in to finish him off."

"*Vaya con Dios*," the don said as Davy wheeled his horse around.

"You folks take care of yerselves," was the Kansan's reply.

"*Adios, Indio,*" said Jesse Santacruz, the sheepherder whose rescue first embroiled Davy and Soaring Hawk in a range war with the wild and woolly Texans. "*Buena suerte*. Good luck, amigos."

The Pawnee nodded, the resolute set of his features never changing. The Kansan waved his hand.

"Kill him good," Hector Mirabal said, slapping the flank of Davy Watson's passing horse.

"Good as I can," the Kansan called back over his shoulder, as he and Soaring Hawk rode out of the little plaza which faced the *hacienda* of the great New Mexican *rico*, Don Solomon Mirabal.

The *hacienda* itself was an appalling sight, having suffered extensive damage when it was under siege by Bill Fanshaw's Texans. Great sections of the long and rectangular, two-storied building's adobe walls had been blown to pieces when the Texans lobbed sticks of the deadly new explosive, dynamite, at the *hacienda*. The explosions had brought fire in their wake, and its ravages showed in smoke-blackened walls and charred beams and window frames. Anyone with an eye for symbols would have likened the bare and gutted *hacienda*, with its blackened burnt sections standing out against the sunlit dazzle of white-washed adobe walls, to a death's head. More than anything, the sight of the Mirabal *hacienda* in the glare of the New Mexican sun brought to the Kansan's mind the image of a skull, picked clean by vultures and bleaching in the desert.

It was with this desolate and forbidding vision in mind that the Kansan turned his face to Texas and rode off the Mirabal spread. The expedition was not to be a lighthearted one, considering the fact that Bart Braden, certainly one of the toughest and deadliest men Davy Watson had ever met, would be fighting on his home ground, in the midst of his fellow-Texans. No, it would not be easy.

Even though Bart Braden's trail was cold by the time that Davy Watson and his blood-brother rode southward in pursuit of him, the Kansan had little fear of losing the ramrod's scent. In the state of Texas, the sight of a male *Anglo* traveling in the company of a young, female *chicana* was a curiosity, an extreme rarity in that segregated society. People would remember such a sight; it would not be difficult to pick up the tracks of such an odd couple. Catching up with Braden would not be the hard part of the Kansan's mission; taking Raquel Mirabal and besting the Texas ramrod *would* be, Davy was certain of that.

Heading due south, and riding far to the west of the new settlement of Roswell, which was a stronghold of the *tejano* cattle interests in the New Mexico Territory, Davy and Soaring Hawk followed the banks of the Rio Penasco eastward from the town of Elk, until they reached its junction with the waters of the Pecos River.

Along the Pecos the two men rode, through Lakewood and Carlsbad, past Otis, Loving and Malaga, crossing Delaware Creek in the Red Bluff country, at the point where the Pecos flows through Texas on a southeasterly course.

Past Orta and Menton, and into the town of Pecos, the Kansan and the Pawnee rode, picking up Bart Braden's trail at that point. From there they followed the course of the Pecos to Sheffield, and then into Crockett County, in West Texas, where they headed eastward over the vast expanse of the Edwards Plateau.

Through Segovia and Fredericksburg, and then due south the blood-brothers rode, through Kerr, Bandera and Medina Counties, securely on the Texas ramrod's trail now, crossing over the line into Bexar County, on the last few miles to the city of San Antonio.

"Ain't gonna be long now," Davy told Soaring Hawk, " 'fore we catch sight of our ol' pal, Bart Braden, once't more."

The stoical Pawnee nodded, leaning over in the saddle to loosen his heavy-caliber Sharps rifle in its boot.

"We kill 'im quick," the brave cautioned. "Braden heap dangerous." He shifted uneasily in the saddle, turning to the Kansan as he did. "Too many Texans. Heap dangerous here, I think."

Davy Watson nodded in agreement with this.

"Yep. I think so, too, ol' son. You're right, there—we gotta kill him quick. That's the best way to deal with rattlers and sidewinders."

Raquel Mirabal and Bart Braden spent most of their waking hours together, for the only time that the ramrod let the beautiful daughter of Don Solomon out of his sight was when he locked her in her room at night, on the second story of Oliver Entwhistle's Exchange on San Antonio's bustling main plaza.

The ramrod continued his strange courtship of Don Solomon's lovely daughter. A proud man—proud even for a Texan, Braden was the epitome of humility when it came to Raquel Mirabal. Once he realized that he had the object of his desire securely in his power, deep in the heart of his home state, the ferocity of Bart Braden's obsession abated, and was replaced by a sudden welling of the tenderest feelings that the hardened and cynical cowpoke had ever experienced.

Flowers, compliments, kindnesses, acts of consideration and attentiveness: these were the constant gifts that the Texan lavished upon the dark-eyed and lissome young beauty. And if she had not been his captive, and he her abductor, it could have passed (at least on Braden's end), for the perfect courtship.

For her part, Raquel was astonished by this side of the Texas iron-man's nature. It was a constant revelation, and led her to consider another form of captivity: the one in which men were hostages to their own codes of behavior; the way that they were the prisoners and victims of their own *machismo*. It was an especially hard form of bondage, and an oppression that men—both *latino* and *gringo*—were far from being able to confront, or even acknowledge, for the most part.

She would bide her time, Raquel told herself. And when her moment came, she would avenge herself upon her *tejano* captor, and then escape back to the New Mexico Territory, back to her home and those whom she loved.

All things considered, apart from the small likelihood of being rescued in Texas, Raquel's lot was not a hard one. While she hated Bart Braden for shooting Davy Watson, the first man to awaken her passionate nature, and for taking her away from her land and people, the young *chicana* was at the same time perversely fascinated by the great transformation of the Texan's character.

He had not laid a hand on her, and had always treated her with the greatest respect, never getting drunk and lecherous, after the fashion of most of the *tejanos* she had observed since their entry into the Lone Star State. He had relieved her of the great fear of violation, that specter of rape and abuse which men have visited upon captive women since time immemorial, and one of the deep, primal sources of female anger.

She was his captive—make no mistake about that—but Bart Braden treated Raquel Mirabal with love and respect, denying her nothing but the one thing she wanted most: her freedom.

It was strange and dizzying to contemplate. In two short weeks, the course of Raquel Mirabal's life had been radically altered. In fact, the lives of many people—her father, brothers, family, neighbors, the *tejano* invaders and the unfortunate Davy Watson—had all been deeply affected by Bart Braden's desperate and precipitate act. But the Texan remained unperturbed by the thought of the consequences of his actions. Men in the grip of an overpowering obsession are rarely reflective, or even rational. And he had succeeded; the ramrod had taken what he came after: Raquel Mirabal was his.

But flesh was flesh, and although Bart Braden treated the young *chicana* with the chaste regard of a medieval troubador, his physical needs and the mounting demands of his addictive love drove him to the arms of the women who waited and worked in the *cantina* across the plaza from Oliver Entwhistle's place.

He had been welcomed with warm and willing smiles by most of the bar girls, but he devoted all of his occasional visits to only one among them. Nydia Ramirez was her name; that was all he knew about her, and actually more than he had wanted to know. She was young, and relatively new to the life of a honkytonk girl, but that was of little import to Bart Braden. What mattered most to the Texan was Nydia Ramirez's close resemblance to Raquel Mirabal. And when he made love to her, he made love to a phantom; and when he spent himself in her arms, the name he called out in the darkness was not Nydia's, but that of Raquel Mirabal.

One night, Braden came back early from the *cantina*. Nydia was having her period, and this did not accord with the Texan's idealized image of her;

53

he did not care to associate blood with Raquel Mirabal. Perhaps this association touched something deep within him, reminding the ramrod of all the blood that had been shed as a result of his obsessive love for Don Solomon's daughter.

Heavy drinking and high-stakes poker were the rule in Entwhistle's Exchange that night, and the denizens of the place were whooping it up mightily as Bart Braden came through the swinging doors, their throats having been well-oiled by increasingly liberal applications of the establishment's spiritous lubricants.

"*O-o-oooh, buf'lo gals, ain't ya comin' out tonight, comin' out tonight, comin' out tonight,*" the piano player sang hoarsely, over the roaring hubbub of the crowd and the discordant clangor of his laboring instrument. "*Buf'lo gals, ain't ya comin' out tonight, to dance by the light of the mo-o-o-ooon?*"

Men were missing the spitoons and splattering their neighbors' boots with the juice of Brown's Mule; men were falling-down-drunk or puking in the streets; men were swearing eternal friendship or glaring about the room in enmity; men were either pining for lost loves or shedding sentimental tears at the memory of their dear, gray-haired, old mothers; some were clustered around the jangling upright, singing raucously, clumsily following the voice of the piano player, baying like spent hounds at the end of a long coon hunt; and others were propped up by the elbows at card tables, seated behind piles of blue and red chips, or scribbling with stubby pencils on crumpled papers, with pale, unshaven faces and doleful countenances, scratching out their markers as they gambled cattle or cabins in a last, desperate attempt to recoup their losses.

The long, polished bar was sticky with the evaporated residue of spilled drinks, the four perspiring bartenders behind it having been far too busy dispensing their wares to stop and apply the bar rag where needed. The air of the big room was thick with the smoke of cheroots, stogies, and cigarillos, a smoke as dense as the atmosphere of a Republican caucus room in the last hour of a deadlocked political convention.

Coming into Entwhistle's Exchange cold sober, the totality of this scene struck Bart Braden as something slightly less elevated than a riot at a county asylum. Shaking his head in disapproval, thrusting drunks right and left out of his path, the ramrod impatiently made his way through the weaving, babbling crowd, heading toward the plush-carpeted stairs which led to his suite of rooms on the honkytonk's upper story.

"*Señor Braden*! *Señor Braden*!" someone screeched in a shrill voice.

The ramrod looked up to the head of the stairs, and saw the old Mexican woman who was one of Entwhistle's chambermaids standing there, wringing her hands and wincing as she called down to him, pale in the face and trembling.

His eyes narrowed as he reached the top of the stairs, towering above her as he studied the old woman's features. Braden saw fear and anguish on her face, and he immediately asked the woman what was troubling her.

"The young *señorita*," she mumbled haltingly,

causing Braden's eyes to suddenly widen.

"What about the young *señorita*?" he asked, urging the frightened woman on.

"Before, she 'ave *fuego*—fire—in room," the woman went on, cringing as she looked up at the big Texan. "So I 'ave to let 'er out—"

"*You let her out*?" Braden said loudly, grabbing the old woman by the upper arms, and shaking her the way a mastiff shakes a rat.

"*Señor Braden—por favor*!" she screamed. "I swear I do to save 'er. But she trick me—is only *fuego* in wastebasket. She push past me, an—"

"Goddammit, you old bitch," the ramrod snarled, shaking the woman again. "You let her go?"

The woman burst into tears as she pleaded for her life, lapsing into Spanish in her confusion. Braden, who spoke sufficient Spanish to understand her, ordered her to tell him where Raquel had gone.

Still sobbing, the woman looked up at the Texan. "*No, no, Señor*," she gasped. "The *senorita* ees steel in room. . .she no go way."

"How come she's still in there?" Braden asked suspiciously, suddenly releasing his grip on the old woman's arms.

The woman gasped and paused to rub her arms and catch her breath. The ramrod's hands were down at his sides, and his fingers fluttered impatiently as he waited for the old Mexican woman to speak.

"Dees man come upstairs—*muy borracho*—him very drunk." Braden's eyes narrowed and his hands became still. "He go after her. The senorita go back an' lock 'erself in room. But thees man, he kick open door, an—''

''Git outta my way!'' Braden grunted suddenly thrusting the old woman aside, causing her to fall to the carpeting which covered the upper story's hallway.

Noiselessly, on tip-toe, the ramrod made his way down the hallway, drawing the Colt .45 from its holster as he did.

When he reached the open door to Raquel Mirabal's room, Braden stood to one side of it, his back to the wall. An instant later he leaned to the side and peered cautiously into the room, his finger on the trigger of his pistol.

The sight which greeted the ramrod's eyes caused them to widen in alarm. The first thing he saw was Raquel Mirabal's bed; and the next thing he saw was Raquel's long-limbed body, draped over it.

She was half-naked, her blouse and underthings having been ripped open above the waist. And the big, grimy hand of a man could be seen fondling the young *chicana's* breast. Braden's face went white as he saw the gag in Raquel's mouth and her arms held over her head on the pillow, her two slender wrists pinioned by the big right hand of the bearded man who held her down.

Grunting and writhing furiously, her legs pinned by the man's ham-like left thigh, Raquel was pale and sweating as she struggled vainly to ward off the giant's amorous advances.

''Kitchy-koo, kitchy-koo,'' the man crooned in his gruff voice as he began to rub his thick beard over Raquel's collar bone, traveling down into the cleft between her full breasts.

57

He said this softly, and was therefore in a position to hear the hammer of Bart Braden's Colt click back with an ominous finality. And at that sudden, chilling, familiar sound, the big, bearded man sat bolt-upright upon the bed and turned his face to the door of the room.

"*Braden*!" he gasped, the color fading from his face as he spoke in a voice thick with disbelief. "*Braden*! *You*!"

The man looked up into the huge mouth of the ramrod's .45, then along its dully gleaming barrel, and into two eyes that looked even harder and colder than the metal of the Colt held out before them.

"Should've told me you was comin' by to pay a call, Sweinhardt," Braden said in a voice as cold as death. " 'Cause I'd've come back earlier, so's to welcome you proper-like, *amigo*."

The big bearded man's face was the color of bleached bones, and he sprang to his feet as if the bed had suddenly caught fire beneath him.

"N-n-now, B-b-bart," the man stammered, the pupils of his eyes dilated to thē size of lentils as he stared into the cavernous maw of the ramrod's six-gun. "Lemme explain," he blubbered, sniffling loudly after he had said this.

"No need to explain, Sweinhardt," Braden replied softly, smiling a tight, grim smile. "You know what they say, *amigo*: 'One picture's worth a thousand words.' "

"N-no, Bart," the giant stammered rapidly, his knees buckling as he heard the second cock of the ramrod's trigger. "I was drunk, Bart—so he'p me, God. I-I-I didn' know this was yer filly—I swear it.

I didn't know. . .what I was about. I—"

Sweinhardt's voice trailed off into an incoherent falsetto whisper as Bart Braden held his big Colt out at arm's length and leveled it at the man's chest.

"Oh, oh, oh," was all that the bearded giant could manage to say, his jaw dropping to reveal his yellowed, snaggle teeth, his eyes wide as he stared into the .45's gaping maw, the eyes of a partridge cornered by an advancing coyote.

"Thanks a heap fer droppin' by, *amigo*," Braden told the petrified man, his voice the voice of an executioner. "But it's time to go."

"O-o-o-ooo-oooh," Sweinhardt croaked, his voice sounding like a door opening slowly on rusty hinges. "O-o-o-oooh. . ."

Booom!

The big Colt discharged with a thunderous report, its blast ringing deafeningly in the room as it reverberated off the walls.

The .45 slug plowed into the meat and bone of the giant's chest with an audible smack, its impact thrusting him backward, to jacknife over the bed.

Bart Braden stared impassively as Sweinhardt's huge, gross body hit the floor with a thump like the sound of a dropped anvil.

Raquel Mirabal was sitting up now and staring at the body of her fallen assailant, totally oblivious to the fact that her beautiful breasts were exposed to view.

But this did not register with the Texan, who lowered his smoking pistol and began to walk across the room, stopping when he stood above the fallen man.

"What t'hell's goin' on here?" a balding, medium-sized man with bushy eyebrows and a Van Dyke beard called out a moment later, as he came to the doorway of the room, hitching up his pants and struggling to put on his gunbelt.

Braden was staring down at Sweinhardt, his .45 held out at at arm's length, pointing directly at the fallen man's big head.

"Jus' defendin' the young lady's honor," the ramrod murmured as his finger began to tighten on the Colt's trigger.

"Now, hold on there, son," the man counseled from the doorway, reaching out a hand toward Bart Braden.

Ba-boom!

The .45 thundered again, and Sweinhardt's head burst open and flew apart, splattering the floor of the room as if it had been an overripe pumpkin dropped from the roof of a barn.

"Now, why'd you have to go an' do a thing like that for?" the man whined, starting to draw his own pistol from its holster. "I'm Cap'n Paul Myers of the State Po-lice, an' I'm a-goin' to have to take you in."

In reply to this, Braden raised his .45 and fired it at the balding man. The impact of the slug sent the state policeman flying backward out of the doorway and smacking into the railing behind him. The wood of the railing parted with a sharp crack, and the man's body shot down to the building's lower story, to land square on top of a poker table below.

Cries of surprise, pain and consternation rose up from the honkytonk's ground floor, as the falling body knocked a man out of his seat and snapped the legs of the table, sending waves of blue, red and white poker chips cascading to the blotter-green carpeting.

"C'mon, honey," Bart Braden gently told Raquel Mirabal, who looked at him with wide, uncomprehending eyes. "We got to light outta here, now."

"*Dos muertes*," she whispered, acknowledging both dead men, while the Texan raised her from the bed and handed her a jacket.

"*Vamanos, muchacha*," Braden whispered softly as, Colt .45 in hand, he led Raquel Mirabal out of the room and down the plush-carpeted stairs, through the confused and milling crowd below, and out into the cool, dark night of Texas.

"Now, looky here, Albert," an old, white-haired man was saying to an old black man, as Davy Watson and Soaring Hawk dismounted in San Antonio's main plaza. "Why is it," the old white man went on, "that you nigrahs allus seems to prefer certain religious sects. What I mean to say is—" here he paused to clear his throat loudly.

The Kansan pretended to adjust the cinch strap on his saddle while he listened with interest.

"What I mean to say is," the old white Texan went on, "how's it that so many of you people is Baptists, Albert? How come that's so?"

The black man straightened up as he sat on the porch of the building next to the Exchange where Davy and Soaring Hawk were hitching their horses, cocked his head to one side, and squinted at the white-haired man.

"You kin read now, cain't you?" he asked the man.

"Well, shore I can read," the white man replied testily.

"Well, I s'pose you's done read the Bible, hain't you?"

" 'Course I done read the Bible!"

"Den you's probly read 'bout John de Baptis', hain't you?" the black man asked.

"Shore I have," the old white man said impatiently. "What of it?"

"Well," the black man said with a triumphant smile, "you hain't never done read 'bout *no John de Methodis'*, now has you?" The white man shook his head. "You see, I gots de Bible on my side, den," the black man crowed jubilantly.

Davy Watson was chuckling as he entered the Exchange. He and Soaring Hawk passed by the bar and headed for a table, having decided to have dinner before they began their search for Bart Braden.

Making the rounds of San Antonio's many Exchanges could be wearing work, the Kansan thought, recalling his pub-crawling escapades in Virginia City, when he was on the trail of Harvey Yancey, the obscene giant who had abducted the three Mudree sisters. There Davy made the acquaintance of the knowledgeable young reporter Marcus Haverstraw, who guided him on a boozy tour of the many saloons flourishing in the place which had grown up following the discovery of the Comstock Lode.

The epic hangover which had followed as a consequence of the first night's work was enough to convince the Kansan that such a quest ought always to be conducted in a spirit of moderation, and on a full stomach. So it was with this in mind that Davy Watson sat down to a big platter of steak, smothered in onions, and home-fried potatoes, backed up by a huge and frothy schooner of beer. Soaring Hawk ate the same food, but had as his drink, being a man who never touched alcoholic beverages, a tall glass of birch beer. This choice of beverage also skirted the painful and embarassing issue of having to be served at a white man's bar. This was a touchy situation at best, and Davy was greatly relieved when he and his Pawnee blood-brother did not have to drink at the bar of whatever saloon or honkytonk to which their business had brought them.

In the background a painoforte played the *Varsoviana*, and the Kansan had a faraway look in his eyes as he remembered hearing that tune in the *hacienda* of Don Solomon Mirabal, seated at a table and gazing into the dark doe-eyes of the *patrón's* daughter, Raquel.

There were a lot of women in the honkytonk, a place whose sign proclaimed it Wilson's Exchange, and many of them were not bad-looking either, the Kansan realized, feeling a surge of heat in his groin.

"Mebbe we ought to rest up a spell," he said, turning to the Pawnee. Whether Bart Braden had molested Raquel or not, the Kansan reasoned, he would surely have done it by now. There was no longer any point in getting worked up on that score.

Soaring Hawk was eyeing the women, too.

"Yep. Mebbe," he grunted, nodding in agreement with this. The bar girls began to stir as they became aware, with the sixth sense developed in their trade, of the two men's interest, fussing suddenly with their gowns and hair, and flashing bright smiles in the direction of the newcomers.

"Yeah, le's knock off fer a couple of hours, an' then git down to business," Davy Watson told the Pawnee brave, as he raised the last of the beefsteak to his mouth.

"Good," the Indian replied with characteristic brevity.

"Well, dammit all, John," Davy heard one of the Texans at the table behind him say as he sat and smiled back at the bar-girls, "that's the way it is with niggers in Mexico. Them darkies livin' down there actually has an advantage over a white American. The greasers likes 'em better, considerin' us Texas folk a mite too rough fer 'em."

"An' well they should," another chimed in gruffly. "We done kicked their butts enough."

The men at the table all laughed loudly.

"But I swear to God A'mighty, its the truth," the first man went on. "A nigger in Mexico is jus' as good as a white man, an' if'n you don't treat him civil-like, he will have yer butt hauled up to court an' fined by some fat ol' *alcalde*. Can you believe that, boys?"

"Well, that jus' says more 'bout the greasers than it do 'bout the niggers," another man commented. "They ain't none too bright. Why, I done heard this from a nigger hisself—a young buck name of Zachariah, who used to be a slave on my Aunt Eulalie's place in Austin. He done tole me

64

that a colored man, if'n he made up his mind to be industrious, could make him a right comfortable livin' down in Mexico.''

"If'n he was in-dust-tri-ous," the first man crowed scornfully, "he wouldn't be no darkie, now would he?''

The men laughed again.

"Well, what this buck done tole me," the other man continued, "was that wages was low, but they had all they earned fer they own. An' a man's livin' didn't cost him much there. Colored men who was in-dustrious an' savin', young Zachariah said, could make money faster'n the Mexicans theyselves—*because they had more sense*! That's what he done tole me.''

"Well," another man grunted, "thar's somethin' to what that boy said, I'll grant you that.''

"By gum, Russell," said another, "that's prob'ly the first time in yer life that you ever done agreed with a nigger.''

The men laughed raucously.

Davy Watson frowned and shook his head. He was disgusted with many of his fellow citizens, whom he considered to be bigots and shirkers, men unworthy of the great ideals of the Declaration of Independence which was their heritage. The stain of prejudice was a deep and enduring blot upon the American character, and the nation's relationship with its Negro citizens was an especially complex and tormented one.

Even Thomas Jefferson, that great libertarian, Davy reminded himself, while engineering the Declaration of Independence and the Constitution of the United States, had been a slave owner himself.

And the man had begotten several mulatto children by his black slave mistress, Sally Hemming. Jefferson loved that woman, the Kansan told himself, and yet he kept her as a slave. This seemed, to Davy, to embody the great racial contradiction in the American character: noble ideals and a reality of racial injustice; fiery speeches in defense of liberty in the halls of Congress, and lynch mobs in the streets. Why even such a liberal city as New York had recently suffered from racial disturbances. During the draft riots of the Civil War, less than a decade ago, a number of the white citizens of that fair city took it upon themselves to hang a number of their darker brothers from the lamp posts.

And of all the bigoted sum'bitches I've ever come acrosst in my travels, the Kansan told himself, a bitter smile coming to his lips, these Texans has got to be the worst. They spit on the rights of darker folk, an' laugh at the Mexicans for upholdin' them.

He shook his head and sighed. Those poor, brown-faced, priest-ridden heathen actually hold, in earnest, the ideas on this subject put forth in that good ol' joke of our fathers—the Declaration of American Independence.

When, he asked himself, were his countrymen going to get their heads out of their asses, and get down to the business of looking each other right in the eye and respecting themselves for what they were. Then the Kansan recalled the lines he had read in one of his Uncle Ethan's books, a volume published only a decade ago, in the year preceeding the civil war. Its author had remarked the persistent flights to Mexico of Negro slaves in Western Texas, and written:

"Brave negro! say I. He faces all that is terrible to man for the chance of liberty, from hunger to thirst to every nasty form of four-footed and two-footed devil. I fear I should myself suffer the last servile indignities before setting foot in such a net of concentrated torture. I pity the man whose sympathies would not warm to a dog under these odds. How can they be held back from a slave who is driven to assert his claim to manhood?"

To do justice to a great number of his countrymen, Davy recalled that there were many of them—male and female—who were committed to the principles of liberty and justice for all. And their time would come, he told himself. . .for if it did not, then the American nation would surely perish, its life extinguished by the rampant spread of the cancers of racism and social injustice.

The Kansan's spirits were suddenly buoyed, and lifted out of that pool of melancholy in which they had been immersed, when his wandering eye met that of a young woman who stared at him from the head of the stairs which led to the Exchange's upper story.

She was tall and auburn-haired, with cornflower-blue eyes, a long, aquiline nose, full, red lips and a strong jaw. Her emerald green gown swelled at the bosom, and again at her hips. The woman was handsome of feature, Junoesque of figure, and in her early thirties, the Kansan opined. He found himself imagining the way her piled auburn hair would look against the pure white of a clean pillow, fanning out to its full length in radial lines, like the rays of the sun on a bronze plaque. She was definitely the most interesting woman Davy Watson had seen since the day he'd first laid eyes on Raquel Mirabal.

Soaring Hawk had also found a focus for his carnal interests, and the Pawnee was staring across the room, the faintest trace of a smile upon his lips.

"See anythin' you like?" Davy inquired.

"Hunh," the Pawnee grunted, nodding at a blonde in a pale blue gown, who smiled back as he did.

"Me too," the Kansan told him. "That there big gal on the stairs has jus' caught my fancy. Let's get to it, ol' son."

A few minutes later, they were ensconced in a suite of rooms on the upper story of the Exchange, the women of their choice beside them on velvet sofas, making polite conversation and drinking champagne. Soaring Hawk had as his drink a birch beer in a tall glass, garnished with thin slices of Texas lemon and lime.

The big redhead called herself Delia Lee, and the blonde, an emigrant from the state of Rhode Island, was named Mary Louise Pringle. Both were possessed of hearty, fun-loving dispositions, and it was not long before the suite's parlor rang with their laughter. The Kansan laughed with them, and even the normally poker-faced Pawnee was soon smiling broadly, an indication, among his people, of great hilarity.

Delia Lee, upon learning of the customs of Soaring Hawk's tribe, and Plains Indians in general, began to relate the views held by one of her "regulars," a man named Jim Primrose, a

68

former member of the famed Texas Rangers.

He was, the redhead told her listeners, an excellent scout and a very reliable man. Orderly, quiet and disciplined, Primrose was pleasant and open, but at the same time restrained and tactful; certainly not your average frontiersman.

The old Ranger spoke Spanish like a Mexican, and had mastered a number of Indian languages, as well as the signs of several tribes. And although he had the frontiersman's hatred for Indians, Jim Primrose gave them credit for patience, endurance, perceptiveness, and generally respected their abilities as outdoorsmen. And, as a first-hand observer of the red man, Primrose had his pet peeve:

"Why do people who write books," he asked in Delia Lee's anecdote, "always make Indians talk in that hifalutin' way they do? Indians don't talk so, and when folks talk that way to them they don't understand it. They don't like it, neither."

Soaring Hawk nodded solemnly as he met the redhead's eyes.

"I went up with Lieutenant Walpole," she continued, mimicking the old Texas Ranger's drawling speech, "when he tried to make a treaty with the Northern Apaches. He had been talking up in the clouds, all nonsense, for half an hour, and I was trying to translate it just as foolish as he said it."

The redhead paused to knock down her glass of champagne. "An old Indian jumped up and stopped me," she said, continuing Primrose's story while holding out her glass to be refilled.

"What does your chief talk to us in this way

for?" Delia Lee went on, now switching to the voice and mannerisms of an old Apache chief. "We ain't babies. We are fighting men. If he has got anything to tell us we will hear it. But we didn't come here to be amused; we came to be made drunk, and to get some blankets and tobacco."

Davy guffawed at this, and the Pawnee broke out into bursts of snorting laughter.

"We ain't babies," Soaring Hawk repeated between snorts, slapping his thigh. "That heap funny. White chief talk to Injun baby, mebbe he get understood."

"You ain't refilled my glass yet, Mr. Wasson," the statuesque redhead told the Kansan reproachfully, still holding out her empty champagne glass.

"Watson's my handle, Miz Delia," he told her. David Lee Watson."

"We got similar names," was her reply, "David Lee an' Delia Lee."

"Just like brother and sister," the Rhode Island blonde said sweetly, with a mischievious glint in her eye.

"Ain't you gon' fill me up, honey?" the redhead asked suggestively, leaning over and exposing her fair and ample bosom to the Kansan.

"I, uh, thought we'd do that inside," Davy told her, his ears reddening as he inclined his head in the direction of the bedroom door.

"Why, I'll jus bet Mr. Watson's heart is already full to overflowing with brotherly love," Mary Louise chimed in again before knocking back her own glass of champagne.

"How long you been on the trail, David Lee?" the redhead whispered in the Kansan's ear, her voice exciting him with its breathy contralto.

"Nigh onto two weeks," he whispered back lustily, suddenly catching the fragrance of her thick, auburn hair.

"You ready to hop back in the saddle, cowboy?" she asked with a wicked smile.

"Sure am," Davy replied. "Been dog's years since I done got the chance to mount such a fine-lookin' filly."

"You've got the look of a hard-ridin' hombre, David Lee," the redhead whispered, coyly lowering her eyes as she did.

"Oh, don't you worry none, Mr. Watson," Mary Louise called out as she plunked herself down on Soaring Hawk's lap. "Ride just as hard as you please. This filly is fully saddle-broke."

They all laughed at this, the Pawnee included. And the couples were still laughing as they retired to their respective bedrooms.

Back in the saddle—Hoo-wee damn! the Kansan thought as the big redhead guided his throbbing rod into her auburn-thatched sex.

He caught his breath as she lowered herself upon him, feeling at every millimeter of penetration the hot, gripping suction of her wet, juicy quim.

Delia Lee squatted over Davy Watson, leaning over and reaching out to rake his hairy chest with long red nails. She began to move from side to side, her hips rotating in churning motions, as she smiled triumphantly down at him, watching the expression on his face through narrowed, cat's eyes.

71

His own eyes were rolled up in their sockets; he puffed and blew as the redhead's churning hips and gripping, sucking pussy ignited a fire in the pit of his groin.

"Ju-da-a-as Priest," he moaned, writhing beneath the redhead who rode and churned above him.

Slurp, slurp, were the wet hungry sounds that her sex made as she jerked her red-muffed pelvis and quickened her stroke, looking down and running the length of the Kansan's shaft, not stopping until her engorged nether lips were butted against the expanse of his groin, flattened and parted and lost to sight in the thick tangle of his pubic hair.

Then suddenly, up again—as she hooked her groin backward and started on the upswing. And then down again—as the Kansan moaned loudly and shook with delight.

Through narrowed eyes, puffing like a steam kettle on the boil, Davy Watson watched the thick swollen lips of the redhead's sex travel their downward, pouting course over the length of his shaft, which was slick and gleaming with the fluids of her own arousal.

Up and down, in and out. His rod came into view, and then suddenly disappeared within those dark, swollen lips, gripped by the hungry orifice which it had penetrated.

Slurp, slurp. Delia Lee stroked and churned. *Up and down. Slurp, slurp. In and out.* She milked him with her hot and gripping pussy, milked him as surely as a Wisconsin dairymaid milks a prize Guernsey. Faster and faster she stroked, leaning

72

forward now, her forearms resting upon his chest and shoulders.

"Judas Prie-e-eest," he moaned, feeling like a volcano about to erupt. "Great God in Sion," were the Kansan's last words, as Delia Lee's artful movements and eloquent organ ransacked his bodily fluids, causing him to cry out between clenched teeth.

"*Heee-e-e-aaah*!" he cried as a stream of jissum shot out of his over-stimulated organ and bathed her sheath in its milky abundance.

"O-o-oooh, Jesus God!" he yelled, his body beginning to jerk uncontrollably in reaction to the overwhelming orgasm he was at that instant experiencing.

"Oh yes, sweet man!" Delia Lee called out, getting into the spirit of things as she lay over him and writhed, her pelvis butted against his.

"Hoo-ooo, hoo-ooo," she began to whimper in response to the swooping, vertiginous rise of her own orgasm, closing her eyes and clenching her even, white teeth.

The redhead whimpered and the Kansan yodeled, with the bedsprings beneath them providing the ground bass for their amorous duet. In the parlor of the suite the vocalizing could still be heard, carrying as far as the door on the opposite side of the room, beyond which Soaring Hawk and the blonde from Rhode Island made love.

Back in Virginia City, the Pawnee had gone to bed with a redhead and had been fascinated to discover that her pubic hair was much the same color as that of her tresses. And now, upon seeing the fleecy blonde muff of Mary Louise, he crowed with delight.

She was only the second white woman that he had ever lain with, and the brave was still acutely titillated by contrast between the blonde's coloring and that of the Indian women he had known.

Mary Louise, as Desirée the redhead before her, had never slept with an American Indian, and also regarded the encounter with a certain amount of excitement.

She found the Pawnee much gentler with his hands than the general run of white men that she had known. He was, as Indians usually were, much less preoccupied with a woman's breasts than were his white brothers, preferring to caress and fondle her in a great variety of places.

Mary Louise's eyes lit up when the Pawnee leaned over her, put his nostrils close to her bare, warm flesh, and began to snuffle like a hound catching the scent of a possum. This was known to learned scholars in the East as the "olfactory kiss," although Mary Louise was unaware of it. It was an ancient custom that had originally come from Asia, and was still practiced there by many an amorous Asiatic.

Being fondled, caressed and thoroughly snuffled, although never kissed, had aroused the blonde, and her juices were flowing copiously as she sighed and squirmed on the bed, while the Pawnee continued to snuffle his way down to the furry delta between her plump white thighs.

Snuffling and poking with his nose like a pig rooting out truffles, Soaring Hawk conveyed to Mary Louise the impression that he wished her to spread her legs.

Wide-eyed and open mouthed, never having been snuffled in that area before, the blonde wonderingly complied with the brave's wishes.

Still snuffling lightly, and ruffling Mary Louise's fluffy, golden muff with the tip of his nose, Soaring Hawk lowered his head as he came to her two pink lips and the shadowy, musk-scented cleft between them.

Lying on her back, eyes round as saucers, her thighs quivering with anticipation, Mary Louise wondered where the Pawnee would poke his nose next. Would he snuffle between her lips? she asked herself, curious to discover what sensation would attend such an act. Or would he actually try to thrust his nose into her vagina, attempting some strange and exotic form of penetration, wherein the nose is substituted for the organ usually preferred in such instances?

"Oooh," she cried in soft, flute-like tones while his nose skimmed over her mount of Venus. "Ooooh."

He did not penetrate Mary Louise with his prominent, Plains Indian's nose, to her commingled relief and disappointment. But what he did instead surprised the Rhode Island blonde even more, for the "savage" from the plains of Kansas and Colorado suddenly began to indulge in a sexual practice which was more characteristic of Frenchmen and other Europeans of a certain level of sophistication than her fellow countrymen.

"Ooo-oooh," Mary Louise whispered, going wide-eyed at the discovery that the American

75

Indian could be adept at oral sex. "Uum, Mr. Hawk," she murmured arching her pelvis up slightly to meet the Pawnee's pursed, questing lips and the tongue which browsed the downy forestation of her pink and musky coozy.

Soaring Hawk tilted his head sharply to one side, and then pressed his thin lips firmly against the fat, pouting nether lips of the blonde, in the only kiss that he would ever bestow upon her.

"Oh, that feels so-o-o good, Mr. Hawk," Mary Louise murmured, squirming in response to the Pawnee's vulvic kiss.

Then she emitted a little gasp, as his tongue entered the cleft between those burning and engorged nether lips and traveled upward in a darting, flicking run.

"Ooo-ooo," she hummed contentedly, stretching out her limbs upon the bed, a blissful smile upon her lips as the brave's tongue circled the base of her erect and sensitized clitoris, and then traveled down to her vaginal orifice.

A little while of this, of the Indian's expert and persistent ministrations, and the Rhode Island blonde was moaning and groaning and writhing in the exquisite, tumescent agony that immediately precedes the release of orgasm.

"Oh, Mr. Hawk. Oh."

"Ugh," the Pawnee grunted, his tongue darting over and around her pink, swollen button the way a gila monster's tongue darts flies off a cactus bud.

In a moment more it was she, and not the Indian, who began to whoop. Mary Louise's body stiffened as her climax broke over her in irresistible waves.

"Oh, my land sakes," she whispered minutes later, after it was all over and she had finally recovered enough to open her eyes and speak. "Oh, that was just peachy, Mr. Hawk."

Mary Louise was full of gratitude as she sat up and leaned over the now recumbent Soaring Hawk, planting ardent kisses upon his pectorals and grasping the shaft of his erect cock the way an Iroquois hefts a new tomahawk.

"Oh, Mr. Hawk," the little blonde said between the moist kisses she smacked along the alley that ran along between Soaring Hawk's pectorals. "That was. . .*so* good. . .now let me. . .make you . . .com-for-ta-ble. . . ."

By the time Mary Louise said this, her kisses had travelled down to the Pawnee's groin, and as if to punctuate her statement, she raised her head, parted her full lips and then leaned forward again, taking the head of the Pawnee's lance in her mouth while she worked over its shaft with her right hand, stroking and twirling with all the expertise of a Pawtucket taffy puller.

"Ugh," the Pawnee grunted as the heat of a Comanche bonfire blazed in his groin. And a few moments later he whooped like an Indian on the warpath, firing off a burst of jism into the Rhode Island blonde's warm and ardent mouth.

It was good to come off the trail, the Plains Indian reflected a few minutes later, falling into the deep, dark sleep that follows gratified desire.

3

Bart Braden's Enemies

"Boy, sure feels good t'git yer ashes hauled after a long spell on the trail, don't it, ol' son?" Davy said to his Pawnee blood-brother as the two men sauntered out of the honkytonk which fronted on San Antonio's main plaza.

The Pawnee had a faint smile of contentment upon his face as he nodded to the Kansan.

"Blonde woman blonde all over," he told him, with the air of a scientist who had just verified the results of an important experiment.

"Ol' Delia Lee got herself in the saddle an' took me for one hell of a wild ride," Davy informed Soaring Hawk. "Why, that lady could git a job in the circus jus' 'bout any time she pleased." He shook his head admiringly. "Best damn bareback rider I ever did see."

"Ride like Pawnee after buffalo, huh?" the grinning brave grunted.

"How 'bout you, my brother? You have a good time?"

Soaring Hawk nodded. "Like deer, I browse in grass. Woman moan like catamount in mating time. Then, when that finished, she come round and puff me like peace pipe." He grinned again.

78

"She smoke 'til pipe empty. Heap good. Heap big medicine."

"Yep," Davy Watson agreed, laughing. "It's medicine like that what'll set ya to rights."

It was then, as the pair made their way down the front steps of the honkytonk, that they noticed the crowd across the plaza, milling in the moonlight, outside of Oliver Entwhistle's Exchange.

"Judas Priest, I wonder what's goin' on over there?" Davy said as they set foot on the boards of the street.

"Must be from shots before. I hear in bedroom. You hear?" Soaring Hawk asked the Kansan.

"Oh, yeah," Davy Watson replied. "I thought that was jus' somebody a-whoopin' it up on a Friday night. You know how wild these Texas boys gits."

"Mebbe somebody shoot somebody," the Pawnee suggested.

"That's a possibility I wouldn't count out," Davy replied, steering the Indian in the direction of Entwhistle's Exchange. "Le's have us a look-see."

"Same old story," the brave told him making a sour face. "White man go to church on Sunday, hear preacher say all men brothers. By Friday, he forget this, get likkered up and shoot brother."

The Kansan nodded and smiled a wry smile. "Judgin' from what you say, I reckon you been around Christian folks a mite."

"Many Christian only Christian on Sunday." Soaring Hawk observed.

"Fella whose book I once read—I fergit his name—said, 'The last Christian died on the cross.' " Davy smiled again. "I know that's a right

79

blasphemous thing to say, but it does make a point.''

"Cross is two logs where Jesus hang?" Soaring Hawk volunteered.

"Yep. That's the point of the story."

Not quite getting the point, Soaring Hawk nodded. "I know story of Jesus. What soldiers do to him make me think of Indian torture. Be like Jesus captured by Apache or Comanche, mebbe."

"He was beat an' crucified by Roman soldiers," Davy told the Pawnee.

"Sound like Indian more than white man."

"Nope. They was white men. Eye-talians, from Italy. That's in Europe, where all the white men come from."

At this point they had crossed the plaza, and were on the street outside of Entwhistle's Exchange.

"Hey, mister," Davy said, tapping the shoulder of a tall man in black who wore pipestem pants, a soft, black felt hat and spectacles whose shape and wire frames reminded the Kansan of pictures he had seen of Ben Franklin. "What's been goin' on in this here place?"

"Dunno exactly," the man said as he turned to face Davy, his eyes widening when he caught sight of Soaring Hawk. " 'Pears that one fella—I knew *him*, big man, ugly ol' sum'bitch name of Sweinhardt—was a-messin' 'round with some other fella's gal."

"That's one of the best ways to get shot that I know of," Davy observed.

"Well, he sure 'nuff did," the man in black went on. "Got his head blowed off, as I heerd it."

"Kinda figgers," Davy muttered, reflecting upon the perils of illicit love in the West. "That ain't the kinda thing a man takes lightly hereabouts."

"However," the man continued, "if ever a man needed shootin', it was that Sweinhardt fella. He was rotten through an' through. Warn't above horse thievin', bushwhackin' or a-cheatin' at cards. An' if'n anybody ever had a good word to say 'bout him, I never done heerd of it. Why, I reckon you could say that puttin' ol' Sweinhardt under ground was doin' the municeepality of San Antone a public service." The man frowned and shook his head. "He was one bad *hombre*, an' we's a heap better off without him."

"Who shot this here Sweinhardt?" Davy asked.

"Ain't learned that yet," the man answered. "But that ain't all. After Sweinhardt got his fat ugly head blowed off, some fella who was in the State Po-lice come an' made ready to arrest the *hombre* what done shot him. But he was quick on the trigger, that *hombre*, an' he got the drop on t'other fella. Shot him too. An' at close range, I reckon. Blowed him right through the upstairs railin', an' sent him a-droppin' smack in the middle of a high-stakes poker game. They was poker chips all over the floor from one wall to the other." The man chuckled.

"An' one galoot got hisself knocked out by the fallin' body," he went on. "An another got two front teeth knocked out by the toe of the dead man's boot."

"Who kilt 'im?" Davy heard someone saying in a raw, angry voice, as two men carried the body of

81

a balding man out through the front door of Oliver Entwhistle's Exchange.

"Ain't nobody talkin', John," another voice replied, off to one side. "But I got me one *hombre* who's a-willin' to tell us what he knows."

Davy and Soaring Hawk looked in the direction of the speakers, and then watched as they came together, one of them dragging a third man along roughly, his fist wrapped in the front of the man's flannel shirt.

"Well, who kilt 'im?" the angry-voiced man demanded once more. Davy saw that he was a brawny man with red mutton-chop whiskers and a big, sandy, handlebar mustache.

Cringing as the second man thrust him forward, the third man put his hands up before his face.

"Speak up, man!" the brawny, mustachioed man roared. " 'Cause patience ain't one of my virtues. If'n you don't start a-talkin', like as not I'll be of a mind to make you. An' if'n I have to do that, why, after I'm through with you, you'll wish that you had been taken by Comanches instead."

The third man whimpered and made choking sounds, apparently having lost the power of speech.

As his eyes traveled over the forms of the man called John and his partner, the Kansan saw that both men wore upon their chests the badge of the Texas State Police.

"Quit whinin' like a hound-dawg tied to a back porch," the brawny man ordered, "or I'll blow off yer earlobes, one at a time." He whipped out a huge Smith and Wesson from his holster and pointed it at the cringing, whimpering man's head.

Davy Watson heard this and winced, the state policeman's words bringing to mind his pistol duel on Mount Davidson, high above a sleeping Virginia City, where he had downed the Alabamian procurer, Malcolm Shove—and had his own left earlobe shot off.

Fingering the scar tissue above the absent earlobe, the Kansan watched the drama unfolding before his eyes.

"Seems like ever' body here'bouts knows who done all the shootin', John," the second man informed his partner. "But nary a soul cares to say. So I figger that perticular *hombre* got him a passel of friends, or else ever'body's jus' plain scairt of him. Or mebbe both."

"But this jasper knows, don't he?" the brawny, redhaired man said loudly, his face reddening as he spoke in tones of impatience. The man in the middle covered his face with his hands and continued to whimper, unable to speak.

"He's a buddy of that Sweinhardt fella," the second man said. "So I don't reckon he cares none fer the *hombre* what shot 'im. I'd say he's our best bet to find out who done gunned down ol' Paul."

Click. The cowering man gasped as the brawny state policeman cocked his big Smith and Wesson pistol.

"You got yerself three seconds, mister, to start talkin' or prayin'."

Davy saw the man's knees buckle.

"Better start talkin', *amigo*," the second state policeman advised, grabbing the man by the shoulders to hold him up.

"*One*," the brawny man said in a low, growling

83

voice, aiming the big gun at the cowering man's head.

"Oooh," the cowering man said in the voice of a baying dog as he fought to regain the power of articulate speech.

"Two."

"Hoo-hoo-woo-oooo," bayed the terrified man in his canine falsetto, still unable to speak.

Davy and Soaring Hawk looked on in great fascination, both of them wondering whether or not the man would get his voice back in time to save his life.

The second state policeman cleared his throat.

"Yiii-i-i-i-iii," the dog-man bayed, tears streaming down his leathery cheeks.

"Don't look like he's gonna come through," the second state policeman said matter-of-factly.

"No, it don't—dadblame it!" the brawny man growled, his thumb going to the hammer of his huge pistol.

Click. The weapon double-cocked loudly, and as it did, the dog-man emitted an eerie, baying wail and fell to his knees on the boards of the sidewalk.

"Three," the brawny man said in a voice as cold as dead men's feet.

"Hoo-oo-ooo, woo-ooo," the kneeling man bayed, still bereft of the power of speech. His tears ran down in torrents, splattering the warped and dusty boards upon which he knelt, and he shook like a man with Saint Vitus' dance.

"Oh, shit," the burly man growled in a voice colored by disappointment. "Ain't nothin' fer it now, but to shoot the sum'bitch."

"Might as well," the second man said in that

84

matter-of-fact voice of his. "Don't look like he'll ever git his voice back, no-ways."

"Yii-yii-yiii!" wailed the dog-man, fully aware that he was kneeling upon death's threshold. "Yii-yiii-I-I. . ."

"Hold on, John," the second man advised. "I think he's a-comin' 'round."

"I-I-I-I. . ." the dog-man persisted.

"Damn well better," the brawny man grumped, tapping the dog-man on the head with the cannon-sized barrel of his Smith and Wesson.

"I-I-I-I'll t-t-talk," the dog-man stammered, finally able to speak. "D-d-don't shoot m-m-me, mister. Please."

"I won't," the brawny man growled, finally lowering his weapon, "if'n I like what I hear."

"Git up, fella," the second man said quietly, nudging the dog-man with his elbow.

Davy Watson and Soaring Hawk exchanged looks as the man rose unsteadily to his feet.

"All right, mister," the brawny man said, "start talkin'. Who done shot ol' Paul Myers?"

The dog-man looked around nervously as a series of angry mutterings arose from the surrounding crowd.

"Don't you pay them no heed, boy," the brawny man said, glaring from face to face with narrowed and angry eyes. "You's got me to answer to. . .as does anybody else what's got a mind to put in his two cents worth."

Nobody in the crowd chose to challenge the angry state policeman.

"Go on, boy," he told the man who had been a crony of the late and unlamented Sweinhardt.

"Let's hear who done the shootin'."

"Fella name of Braden," the dog-man yipped, as a chorus of angry murmurs arose from the crowd. "Bart Braden, I think it were."

"Now, simmer down, folks," the second state policeman cautioned, as the Kansan's jaw dropped and his eyes went wide.

"Bart Braden!" Davy Watson cried out loudly in surprise, suddenly stilling the buzzing hubbub of the crowd.

"What's it to you, *amigo*?" the brawny state policeman growled, impaling the Kansan upon his steely glance.

"Why, I'm after Bart Braden, myself," Davy told the Texan. "Sum'bitch shot me, too."

The crowd began to buzz angrily at this.

"Simmer down!" the second state policeman ordered, whipping out his sidearm and punctuating his command by firing two shots into the air. Immediately following this, the crowd fell silent.

The brawny man looked the Kansan up and down. "Well, if'n you got yerself a score to settle with that fella, then y'all's welcome to ride after 'im with us."

His eyes traveled from Davy to Soaring Hawk. "This here Injun with you, mister?" he asked testily, his eyes narrowing when he saw the scalping knife in the Pawnee's belt.

"Sure is," Davy replied empthatically. "My buddy here's a Pawnee, an' a true friend to the white man."

"Round these parts, an' up north by the Red River," the smaller state policeman told Davy, "we spent us a lotta time fightin' Injuns. How'd you git friendly with this one?''

"This man an' his tribe comes highly spoke of," Davy shot back, his face now as devoid of expression as the Pawnee's. He was learning to keep his feelings in check at critical times in his life, times such as this one.

"Me'n him was together with Colonel Forsyth, at the battle of Beecher's Island," Davy told the two men, flashing them a grim smile as he recalled the encounter at Arikaree Creek in Eastern Colorado, wherein a force of fifty scouts and traders, under the command of George A. Forsyth, withstood a combined mounted force of nearly one thousand Cheyenne, Arapahos and Kiowas.

The men looked impressed; the Battle of Beecher's Island, as the stand came to be called, was celebrated from Maine to California, having inflamed the popular imagination.

"An' his people scouts fer Major Frank North," Davy went on, taking advantage of the impression his words had made.

"Zat so?" the brawny man rumbled, looking the Pawnee over from head to toe. Frank North was already on his way to becoming a legendary figure for his work with the Pawnees. Under his leadership, they had been able—for the first time, to win several decisive victories over their hereditary enemies, the Cheyennes.

"His name's Soaring Hawk," Davy told the two men, "An' he's as good a man as you'll ever be likely to meet. . .which is a thing he'll prove if'n you ever git in a tight spot with him."

The two Texans exchanged questioning looks.

"My name's Watson," the Kansan told them.

"I'm out to git a young lady that Bart Braden done took away from her daddy, up in the New Mexico Territory. An' when I get her back safe-like, I aim to settle that *hombre's* hash—once't an' fer all."

"Well, Mr. Watson," the brawny, mustachioed man said, pausing next to clear his throat. "You'n yer Injun buddy here—"

"Soaring Hawk," Davy interjected.

"Uh, yep. Soaring Hawk," the man went on. "You'n him's welcome to ride along with me'n my friend, here." Saying this, he indicated the smaller man with a jerk of his thumb. The other nodded at Davy and Soaring Hawk. "For we mean to track down this here Bart Braden, an' see that justice gits done."

"You gonna go outta state after him, if'n you got to?" someone asked from the doorway of the Exchange.

The brawny man turned, as did the others and looked the newcomer over. He was a tall bald-headed man, slender except for a "beer belly."

"Now, jus' who might you be, mister?" the brawny man asked, annoyance further roughening his voice.

"I'm Oliver Entwhistle," the man told him, meeting the state policeman's glance. "I own this here place. An' Bart Braden's my friend."

"Well, I hope you done got a chance to say g'bye," the smaller man said sarcastically. " 'Cause I don't spec' y'all gon' see much of him after this."

"You gonna see he gits a fair trial, if'n y'all catch him?" Oliver Entwhistle asked, glaring at the two men.

"We'll take care of ever'thin', mister. Don't fret yerself 'bout it."

"State po-lice cain't never be trusted," the owner of the exchange said angrily, drawing himself up to his full height and staring over the heads of the two men.

"Well, ain't that a crock of shit!" the brawny man retorted angrily, his beefy face going red. "We's Texas Rangers first an' foremost. An' that's how we'll deal with Bart Braden when we git holt of 'im—as Texas Rangers."

"Well, you two is State Po-lice now," Oliver Entwhistle persisted.

The smaller man flicked his badge with his thumbnail. "The State Po-lice is full of scoundrels, shore 'nuf. But that don't mean me'n ol' John here is scoundrels, too. 'Cause we ain't. We's Rangers, through an' through."

"Yeah, but—" Entwhistle began.

"Never mind makin' no argument, mister," the brawny man interrupted, shooting the owner of the honkytonk a hard look. "Braden done gunned down our buddy, an' we aim to run 'im to ground fer that. Now, why don't you jus' mosey back inside, an' wipe down yer bar?"

He said the last sentence in a menacing growl, and his hand was now hovering over the handle of his Smith and Wesson.

Oliver Entwhistle's eyes traveled down to the brawny man's hand. "Y'all ain't man enuf to take Bart Braden," he growled, stepping back and closing the door as he did.

The brawny man spat contemtuously upon Entwhistle's door. Then he turned back to Davy

Watson and Soaring Hawk.

"Well, Mr. Weston," he began.

"Watson," Davy said patiently.

"Uh, yeah. Watson. Like I done said afore, you'n yer friend's welcome to join me'n my partner here."

"We'd be right glad to do that, mister," Davy replied holding out his hand.

"John B. Loudermilk's my name," the brawny man rumbled, pumping the Kansan's hand vigorously. "An' my pal here's T.C. Pritchett."

"Pleased to meet ya," the small man with the pinched and weathered face said quietly, as he offered Davy his hand.

As they shook, the brawny man slowly reached out his hand to Soaring Hawk. The Pawnee met his eye, and after a moment had passed, they shook hands. Then Soaring Hawk and the smaller man shook hands.

"Well," the brawny man said, looking toward the hitching post that stood in front of Oliver Entwhistle's Exchange, "let's go git that sum'bitch."

Realizing that traveling in the company of a lovely young *chicana* presented an unnecessary risk in the western and southern parts of Texas, Bart Braden now made his way eastward through the Lone Star State. Raquel Mirabal rode at his side, casting sidewise glances at her abductor from time to time.

Leaving San Antonio by way of the heights where the neglected Alamo stood, the ramrod headed east, crossing the Guadalupe River at Seguin. From there he went to Lulling and Lockhart, working his way northward to the city of Austin.

Since he had gunned down a state policeman, Braden figured that someone would be coming after him, either a sheriff's posse or a band of the generally corrupt and incompetent Texas State Police. Either prospect did not particularly disturb him, for Raquel had proved to be an excellent rider, and had so far been able to keep up with him under all conditions.

This ability greatly impressed the Texan, and served to increase the intensity of his already super-charged emotions where the young *chicana* was concerned. Courteous, gentle and respectful, both loving and admiring in manner, Bart Braden continued to ply his strange and elaborate courtship. It was a complete turnabout for him: the man who had always stopped at nothing in order to get what he wanted, the man who had been the lover of Bill Fanshaw's daughter, Samantha, and the cattle baron's heir apparent, wooed the daughter of Don Solomon Mirabal with all the patience, delicacy and feeling of a Romantic poet.

While she still considered herself Braden's captive, the Latin beauty gradually became aware of the tender nature of the ramrod's feelings toward her. Raquel had already been much impressed by the way she had been treated—and protected—by the man who had forcibly taken her from the *hacienda* of her father. She was, Raquel had to admit to herself, not unimpressed by the Texan, despite the fact that he represented nearly everything she had been taught to hate and despise.

He was extraordinarily competent—a man who

could do anything that he set his mind to do; and it would be done well, there was no question about that. The Texan had a mind which worked with lightning-like rapidity, a mastery of manual and outdoor skills, the coordination and agility of an athlete, considerable expertise in the use of weapons, iron determination, and a temperament to which fear was a total stranger.

Braden was tall, well-built and handsome, too, the young *chicana* had to admit that. The Texan's thick curly hair, broad sideburns and square jaw gave him a dashing look. All her *amigas* at the convent school of Our Lady of Guadalupe would have remarked that the tall and broadshouldered *tejano* was a fine-looking man. And he walked with the grace of a puma, and had a deep, knowing look in his eye, one which had convinced Raquel that Bart Braden would surely be a most knowledgeable and expert lover.

Indeed, Raquel told herself ruefully, her *tejano* captor was a man of character, ambition, and great ability. Not many men would have presumed to attempt to defy one of the great Texas cattle barons and steal the daughter of a great New Mexican *rico* from right under his nose.

Oh, make no mistake about it, Raquel Mirabal conceded grudgingly, Bart Braden was a bold and fearless man. Few men would have dared ignite a range war merely for the express purpose of abducting a woman.

He was ruthless, as well, Don Solomon's daughter reminded herself, a sudden wave of reproach rising in her heart. He had gunned down her rescuer. Did she not, with her own two eyes, see

Davy Watson's dead body sink beneath the cold waters of that faraway mountain lake? Did not Bart Braden kill the very man who had been her first lover?

Yes, he had, Raquel was forced to admit. That deed, plus the act of abducting her from her father's house, stealing her away from the friends, land and family she loved, had earned the Texan her undying hatred. She would, the young *chicana* reminded herself, get her revenge when the opportunity presented itself. The honor of the Mirabal family would be upheld, make no mistake about that.

What she was forced to admit, having by now spent a considerable amount of time in the company of her *tejano* abductor, was that Bart Braden was a fair man. From what she now knew of him, Raquel was certain that the Texas ramrod was no backshooter or bushwacker. Nor was he a hired killer, *un asesino*.

No, he was a man of honor—that much she would say for him. Hard, determined, even ruthless. Yes, he was that, but he was not a skulking coward; nor was he a man likely to cringe before any opponent, no matter how formidable. In many ways he reminded Raquel of her father.

There had been, she recalled, an exchange of shots during that deadly encounter in the pines by the side of the mountain lake. Each man had fired off several shots. That was proof positive that poor Davy Watson had got a chance to fire back at the man who gunned him down.

At least she could not reproach Braden with cowardice. No, there was honor in the way he had taken her. Raquel thought about the *corridas*, the popular ballads sung by her people, and of the romantic tales of outlaws such as Elfego Baca and Joachim Murietta, the "Robin Hood of the West."

In many of those tales, men had gone against great odds in order to ride off with the women they loved. And that was one more thing that Raquel had to admit: Bart Braden certainly did love her—with a passion that appealed perhaps, more to the eighteen-year-old *chicana* than to an *Angla,* of the same age even though its excesses had bred a series of disastrous consequences.

Pasión. Pasión. Pasión.

The minds of the young girls at the convent school of Our Lady of Guadalupe, at Albuquerque, were consumed by the thought of a passionate love affair. Nearly all of them entertained elaborate fantasies of bold lovers who would come, surmounting all obstacles, and then ride off into the sunset with them. And Raquel Mirabal was no exception.

The circumstances of her abduction and the handsome appearance of her abductor would have driven her former classmates wild with envy, Raquel told herself, now that she had attained a certain perspective on the events which had so radically altered her life.

Ramona Vasquez was betrothed to Julio Santana, a dull and colorless civil servant. Conchita Alvarez would soon wed fat Pepe Guzmán, son of the *patrón*, Don Francisco Guzmán, one of her father's neighbors. Maria Fernandez was being courted by Olivio Ramos, a balding middle-aged merchant. And Raquel Mirabal's best friend, Lucecita Suarez, was being courted by Oscar Aponte, a skinny Albuquerque undertaker.

None among them could match in their wildest imaginings the reality of Raquel Mirabal's daily life. Here she was, having gone from the arms of one bold and handsome man to another. And the second, Bart Braden, that reckless and astonishing man, had killed the first—Davy Watson of Kansas, the man who had touched the lovely *chicana's* heart and made her perform the act of love with him for the first time in her life—and on horseback, no less! *Caramba*! How sad! How beautiful! How exciting!

Who would believe it all? Raquel Mirabal asked herself, as she and Braden caught sight of Austin in the distance. It was all too incredible; that's what everyone would say when they heard her story. But yet, it is a well-known fact that truth is stranger than fiction.

"Won't be long now, 'til we git to Austin, honey," Bart Braden said in his deep and resonant voice, drawing Raquel out of her reverie.

A tiny, reversed Washington was what one celebrated traveler had called Austin, that handsome city on the left bank of the Colorado River. The capital of Texas, Austin's limestone capitol building stood high on a hill, overlooking the general expanse of the city. And from this magnificent cream-colored edifice, a broad avenue ran down to the river, its sides dotted with the major stores and buildings of the municipality.

Buildings of all sorts co-existed in Austin, from

the log cabins of the first inhabitants to the quarried limestone of the municipal buildings and the homes of the well-to-do. Cottages and meaner dwellings were located well back from the main avenue.

The capital of Texas boasted a great number of drinking and gambling places, but not a single bookstore. Churches were rarely to be seen, and Raquel Mirabal shook her head when she considered the question of culture in the Lone Star State. The daughter of the New Mexico *rico* had been schooled in the high culture of Renaissance Spain, having read extensively the works of Cervantes, Calderón, Lope da Vega, and others. She seriously doubted that the vast majority of the *tejanos* could even read at all. . .or do more than make an "X" where their names were required on documents.

"I reckon we can rest here a spell, honey," Bart Braden told Raquel Mirabal as they reined in their horses before a hotel. The ramrod said this confidently, ignorant of the fact that Davy Watson, Soaring Hawk, and two former Texas Rangers were riding out after him.

4

With the Texas Rangers

As Bart Braden had reckoned, the sight of a *gringo* riding in the company of a beautiful young *chicana* was one of the more unusual sights of the southerly part of Texas, and it was not long before the ramrod's pursuers had picked up his trail.

John B. Loudermilk and T.C. Pritchett, the two state policemen who considered themselves Texas Rangers in eclipse, went straight to the Mexicans among the onlookers outside Entwhistle's Exchange, saying that Braden had stolen Raquel from her father's *hacienda*. In this manner, they soon determined which way the fugitive pair had gone. And from the Mexican residents of Alamo Heights, Davy and his companions learned that Braden and Raquel had headed toward the Guadalupe River.

The state policemen were an interesting pair, the Kansan soon discovered, as his trailmates began to tell him about their years of service as Texas Rangers, first to the Republic, and then to the Lone Star State.

Where John B. Loudermilk was big and brawny, T.C. Pritchett was short and sinewy; where the first was loud and garrulous, the second was soft-spoken and taciturn.

The two men, as different as mountain and prairie, were inseparable friends who had served together for many years as Texas Rangers. Paul Myers, the man whom Bart Braden had shot, had also been a close friend of the pair; they had served under him in the Rangers, as well as in the Texas State Police. They rode out in the name of friendship to avenge the killing, vowing not to come off the trail until Bart Braden had been run to earth.

"He's a mighty tough customer," Davy told the two men. "I tangled with him afore."

T.C. Pritchett pursed his lips and let fly an enormous job of tobacco juice, which splattered against a big rock by the side of the trail.

"We's used to dealin' with tough *hombres,* Mr. Watson," he told the Kansan. "Used to come up agin 'em all the time in the Rangers."

"How come you ain't Rangers now," Davy asked, "seein' as how you talks so good about 'em?"

Pritchett shook his head and shifted the huge quid of chewing tobacco to the other side of his mouth. "Ain't no more Texas Rangers, these days," he said tersely.

"How's that?" Davy asked.

"Ol' T.C.'s a man of few words," John B. Loudermilk told the Kansan. "What he means is that the Rangers done got disbanded once't the war twixt the states was over."

" 'At's right," Pritchett muttered.

"Texas was under military control 'til last year, an' the Fed'ral Gov'ment warn't 'bout to let the state organize no bodies of armed men, nohow. So that 'pears to be the end of the Texas Rangers." He sniffed and wiped his nose on the sleeve of his buckskin jacket.

"Then ol' F.J. Davis jus' got hisself 'lected Governor of Texas—that carpetbaggin' sum'bitch—an' figgered if'n he was a-gonna stay in office, he done better git him some way to control the people."

"I don't git yer drift," Davy told him.

"Tell 'im 'bout the 'lection, John," prompted the laconic Pritchett.

"Oh," the brawny, mustachioed man said. "Sure 'nuff. S'cuse me. Y'see, the onliest way a carpetbag Ree-publican could ever git elected was by the Fed'ral Gov'ment taking the vote away from them who was Confed'rates, an' friends of Confed'rates, an' givin' that vote to all the nigrahs what done got freed after the war."

Davy had heard of this tactic, which had outraged the defeated Southerners, and was partly responsible for the birth of that mysterious and menacing new organization, the Ku Klux Klan. This mass disenfranchisement was followed by outrageous political corruption, and the scandal of the carpetbaggers.

"The State Po-lice," John B. Loudermilk went on, "was F. J. Davis's way of keepin' hisself in office, 'cause he ain't 'zackly the mos' popular Gov'nor Texas ever done had."

"Not by a longshot," T.C. Pritchett agreed.

"State Po-lice is brand new," the brawny man continued, "but it already looks to be full of scoundrels an' bullies an' backshootin' dogs. Me'n ol' T.C., why we don't hold with such doin's. We didn' know what we was a-gittin' into, an' we ain't so sure that we wants to have our good names associated with a or-ga-nee-za-tion like this here one.''

"Cain't be doin' us no good, we figger," Pritchett seconded.

"But someday, they's gonna be Texas Rangers once't more," Loudermilk said emphatically, "an' that's what we's a-hangin' 'round fer."

Pritchett nodded. "It's what we's cut out fer."

"But this here State Po-lice business is a big crock o' shit," the brawny man growled. "Why ever'where we rides, folks is allus a-lookin' at us like we done come to rob 'em blind, or bushwhack 'em first chance we git."

Pritchett seconded this by making a sour face and nodding.

"Sounds like a passel of rogues an' scoundrels," Davy Watson observed.

"An' that's puttin' it in a good light," John B. Loudermilk told him, scowling like a fighting terrier entering the pit.

"But the Rangers was another pot o' stew," the big redhead sighed. "We done a job o' work in that here outfit, an' some mighty deeds which folks still remembers."

"We was tough customers, Mr. Watson," T.C. Pritchett told Davy. " 'Cause a Texas Ranger could ride like a Mexican, trail like a Injun, shoot like a Tennessean, an' fight like a devil."

"As ol' Cap'n L.H. McNelly (who was skinny as a rail, had the con-sump-tion, an' never done weighed more than 135 pounds, soakin' wet) said," added John B. Loudermilk, " 'Courage is a man who keeps on a-comin' on.' "

"What he done meant," Pritchett explained, "was that you might be able to slow down an *hombre* like that, but they's no way in hell you're gon' whip 'im. For the man what keeps on a-comin' on is gonna git there hisself, or damn shore make it possible fer the next *hombre* to git there."

"They's a pome 'bout the Texas Rangers," Loudermilk told Davy and Soaring Hawk. "It goes like this:

" 'The stars have gleamed with a pitying light
On the scene of many a hopeless fight,
On a prairie patch or a haunted wood
Where a little bunch of Rangers stood.

They fought grim odds and knew no fear,
They kept their honor high and clear,
And, facing arrows, guns, and knives,
Gave Texas all they had—their lives.' "

"Beautiful pome, ain't it?" asked Pritchett. "Fella name of W.A. Phelson done writ it."

"Them's fine words," the Kansan agreed.

" 'Member ol' Rip Ford?" Pritchett said to Loudermilk. "Back in '58, when we done taught the Comanch' a lesson they never fergot."

"Tell 'em 'bout it, T.C.," the big man urged.

"Shucks, John," Pritchett said, shifting uncomfortably in his saddle and looking down at the trail, his face flushing to a deep, beet-red color. "You tell 'em."

"Ho, ho," the big man laughed as he gazed

warmly, at his buddy. "Sometimes I fergit that ol' T.C. aint' much fer talkin' 'round strangers." He shook his head. "Why, when we's on the trail on our own, he chatters like a blackbird. Cain't hardly shut 'im up. It's me who's the quiet one, then."

"Go on an' tell 'em, John," Pritchett mumbled, still blushing furiously.

"Right," his mustachioed partner said, turning in his saddle to face Davy Watson and Soaring Hawk. " 'Twas back in '58, like I done said, an' ol' Rip Ford—Major John S. Ford, properly speakin'—got the order from Governor Hardin R. Runnels to pertect the frontier."

He paused to clear his throat, hawk up a gob of phlegm, and spit it out on the side of the trail, after which he resumed his story.

"Ol' Hardin Runnels got hisself elected only a few months afore, an' he was determined to make his mark. An' jus' 'bout the best way to do that were to straighten things out somewhat on the Texas frontiers.

" 'I impress upon you the necessity of action an' energy,' " Loudermilk said in an exaggerated manner, as he impersonated the former governor of Texas. " 'Follow any and all trails of hostile or suspected Indians you may discover, and if possible, overtake an' chastise them, if unfriendly.' "

Pritchett, no longer red in the face, began to chuckle loudly.

"That's what he done writ," Loudermilk informed his listeners, chuckling now himself. "He was a fancy-talkin' man."

"I reckon," Davy agreed, smiling. Beside him

rode Soaring Hawk, who wore his usual Pawnee deadpan and seemed unaffected by the performance.

"So ol' Rip Ford, he done went on a campaign up north, in April of '58, with four detachments of Texas Rangers and their allies, the friendly Tonkaways, Anadarkos, an' Shawnees from the Brazos Reserve. Me'n ol' T.C. was there with 'im, an' we left the Red River an' lit out fer a branch of the Washita, where we was well out of Texas, an' deep in Comanche territory."

The Kansan's eyes narrowed as he remembered the close call that he'd had with Pahanca's Comanches in the southern part of the New Mexico Territory. They were a wild and dangerous bunch, without equal as fighters on horseback, and even the dreaded Apaches steered clear of them.

" 'Bout the tenth of May," John B. Loudermilk went on, "our Injun scouts come across't a buffalo carcass what had a couple of Comanche arrows still in it. An' the day after that, they done seen a passel of Injuns runnin' an' killin' some other buffalo. They tole by the tracks of the ponies where the Injuns done set up camp."

He paused to hawk up another mouthful of phlegm and spit it out.

"Next mornin', we done hit the camp—all 215 of us," the brawny ex-Ranger went on. "The Tonks demolished five lodges by the time we rid in an' took 'em some prisoners an' a heap of Comanche ponies. Two of the devils escaped and took off fer the Canadian River. Well, we tore ass after them bucks—all of us, Rangers an' Injuns—an' run three mile after 'em, when what d'ya suppose we done seen?''

"More Injuns, I 'spect," was Davy's response.

"You bet yer boots, more Injuns," John B. Loudermilk replied emphatically. "We done topped this ol' hill, an' seed a mess o' tepees on the far side of the Canadian. Turns out it was the main Comanche camp."

"Tha's right," Pritchett mumbled after letting fly a jet of saliva and Brown's Mule.

"But them sum'bitches was warned by the ol' boys we took off after," the big man continued. "An' when we come down towards 'em, they come toward us at the same time, led by a tough ol' buzzard name of Iron Jacket, who the Comanches figgered to be downright bullet-proof."

Davy recalled the great massed charge of a thousand mounted Indians at the Battle of Beecher's Island, which was led by the notorious Roman Nose, a chief who had also enjoyed a reputation for invulnerability. . .until that charge, the Kansan recalled, when one or more of George A. Forsyth's brave and gallant little band—among them, Eli Zigler, Sigmund Shlesinger and other renowned scouts—brought the Cheyenne down, never to rise again.

"Man ain't been born yet what's bullet-proof," Davy told the two Texans.

"Well," Loudermilk went on, "the Comanch' made themselves a big noise 'bout ol' Iron Jacket bein' that way. He had him this purty ol' shingled an' glitterin' coat of mail—he done got it from a Spanish fella, I fergit how—an' he sure 'nuff looked bullet-proof, covered from crotch to chin with all that overlappin' steel plate he wore."

T.C. Pritchett spoke up while the other Ranger paused to wipe his nose on his sleeve once more.

"Danged if'n we didn't think t'would take a blacksmith to bring 'im down."

Davy and John B. Loudermilk laughed loudly at this comment. Soaring Hawk's expression was as stony and inscrutable as ever while he stared at the small Texan.

"So on they come," Loudermilk resumed, "led by ol' Iron Jacket, who looked like a runaway boiler off'n some Mississippi paddleboat. An' they were all kinds of Comanch' behind 'im, a-whoopin' an' a-screechin' like the devil on a tear."

The Kansan nodded. "Comanches is mighty hellacious Injuns."

"That's fer shit-sure," the Texan agreed. "Well, anyway, ol' Iron Jacket, he rid towards us like a bat out of hell, bringin' that horde of caterwaulin' Comanch' with 'im.

"All of a sudden five or six rifles fired from our side, an' ol' Iron Jacket's horse goes down, a-throwin' the rest of the Comanch' into turmoil an' confusion."

"His horse certainly warn't bullet-proof," chuckled T.C. Pritchett.

"No, sir, nor was that ol' chief," his partner told Davy and Soaring Hawk excitedly. "Rifle balls was a-plunkin' an' a-clangin' as they struck that there coat of plate mail—from where I was it sounded like someone peein' on a tin roof—an' Iron Jacket spun around, teetered this way an' that fer a spell, an' then hit the ground, soundin' as if a mess o' boiler plates had fell off'n a Conestoga

105

wagon."

"He wasn't bullet-proof no more," Pritchett mumbled gleefully.

Loudermilk continued his narrative. "Jim Pockmark, the Anadarko captain, an ol' Doss, one of our Shawnee guides, done claimed the honor of puttin' Iron Jacket away. They was a bunch of holes in the ol' boy's boiler plate, so any number of fellas might've done it.

"The charge broke, an' the battle done fanned out at that point, 'til it covered a circuit more than six mile long by three mile wide. From time to time the Comanch' would try to rally an' make a stand, but we was jus' too much fer 'em."

"Men cussin', women screamin', Injuns hollerin', children a-cryin'," Pritchett added. "If'n you was to die an' go down to hell, I shorely doubt you'd hear anythin' wuss'n that."

"At that point, the Comanch' sent in another chief—never did find out who the fella was," Loudermilk informed his listeners. "An' he led a charge on our flank, where the friendly Injuns was gathered, but ol' Chul-le-que, the Shawnee cap'n, shot the devil off'n his pony. Shortly after that, we druv the rest of 'em off—them that was still alive—which warn't a whole hell of a lot."

"Guess that took care of 'em, huh?" Davy Watson asked.

"T'warn't over yet," T.C. Pritchett said, after sending a gob of tobacco juice whizzing past his horse's ear. "Tell 'em, John."

"We done chased them other Injuns until our horses couldn't take no more—why, they was lathered up like they was 'bout to get a shave. Then

106

we rid back to the Injun camp an' began to divvy up the spoils.''

He wiped his nose on his buckskin sleeve. "But that warn't all," Loudermilk said, sniffling as he withdrew his sleeve. "Turns out there must've been another Comanch' camp 'bout three or four mile up the Canadian, an' them sum'bitches got roused by all the commotion we done whipped up kickin' ass, an' made as if they was a-gonna charge us."

"They was up on this ol' hill," Pritchett told Davy and Soaring Hawk, "a-hootin' an' a-hollerin' like a wolf pack catchin' sight of a flock o' sheep."

"Oh, they was a-yippin' an' a-yappin' to beat the band," John B. Loudermilk seconded, "an' screechin' all sorts of Injun abuse at the force of Tonkaways, Anadarkos an' Shawnees who come with us from the Brazos Reserve."

"Comanch' is wild sons o' bitches," T.C. Pritchett added gleefully. "An' they don't care none fer Reserve Injuns—does they best to wipe 'em out whenever they can."

"But them ol' boys from Brazos warn't no push-overs their own selves," the brawny ex-Ranger said, picking up the thread of the narrative without missing a stitch. "An' they tol' young Lieutenant Shapley P. Ross, who was a-leadin' the Reserve Injuns, to tell ol' Rip Ford that they was a-gonna draw out them Comanch' an' that us Rangers ought to stay in line an' git ready to back 'em up, if the need should arise."

"Them Comanches is sure full of fight," Davy said, his voice accompanied by the creak of leather as he shifted in his saddle.

"Oh, they's a bunch o' shitkickers, all right," the smaller of the two state policemen replied, his shyness disappearing in his excitement.

"So," his brawny, mustachioed partner went on, "the Comanch' began to come down from that there hill. An' as they come, they tried to draw out the Reserve Injuns, a-hopin' to git them so angry an' excited that they'd lose they heads an' jus' go after them, without no thought of strategy nor safety."

"You should've seen it," Pritchett piped up. "Them Comanch' was a pourin' over the hill, callin' the other Injuns every kind of cussword they could think of, makin' faces like the booger man, shakin' they fists an' lances, a-tryin' to git our Injuns all worked up."

"I seed this here book, once't," John B. Loudermilk reflected, " 'bout knights in armor a-chargin' an' a-knockin' each other off they horses. An' y'know somethin?" he asked rhetorically. "Them Injuns mixin' it up shore reminded me of them there knights of old."

"Yep. I seen pitchers like that," the Kansan told the ex-Ranger, recalling his Uncle Ethan's library.

"I reckon that's what it was like," Loudermilk confirmed. "They was shields an' lances, bows and' fancy headgear, horses a-prancin', an' feathers flappin' in the breeze like pennants at some courtly tournament of old.

"Durn battle looked like knights mixin' it up, too. If t'warn't fer the occasional crack of a rifle, a body'd think he was on some ol' battlefield in the days of yore." He sighed.

"All that mixin' it up was nice an' showy, but it

didn't count fer a hell of a lot. Them boys stabbed an' jabbed, cussed an' whooped, an' fired off arrows fer 'bout half an hour, without neither side doin' a whole lot of damage to the other.''

"Then it was time to send in the Texas Rangers," T.C. Pritchett said. "But the Comanch' done backed off, and' quit the field.''

"But we took off after 'em," Loudermilk said in turn. "An' the fightin' got kinda general between us an' the Reserve Injuns agin' that mess of Commanch'. We whupped 'em ever' time met 'em. This went on 'till it was nigh on to two o'clock.

Now, you got to 'member we-all been goin' at it since seven that mornin'. So by the time we druv off that last pack of Comanch', we was all plumb tuckered out—men an' horses together."

Pritchett spoke again. "Why, then we done heard that ol' Buffalo Hump was only twelve miles away with *another* big bunch of red devils—uh, s'cuse me," he said suddenly, going red in the face as he looked at Soaring Hawk. "They, uh, was more *hostiles* there 'bouts," he went on, now staring at the toes of his boots. "But we was all jus' too wore down to light out after 'em.''

"But we done got what ol' Rip Ford sent us after," the brawny man added, beaming proudly at the Kansan and Soaring Hawk. "Ol' Rip, he figgered we done mixed it up with more'n three hunnerd Comanch' that day. An' the Rangers done kilt seventy-six of 'em. An' we captured more'n three hundred horses—''

"That got their goat," T.C. Pritchett chuckled. "Comanch'd druther stop a bullet then have to travel on foot. Why, them big-headed, barrel-chested, bandy-legged little fellas might be the slickest horse riders you ever done seen, but they ain't worth a hoot in hell on foot, I'll tell you that much!''

"Yep," his partner went on. "We done even took us eighteen prisoners, women an' children mainly. An' do you fellas know somethin'? All what the Texas Rangers lost was two men. Now, how 'bout that?" he crowed.

"That there's the gospel truth he's a-tellin' you boys," T.C. Pritchett affirmed.

"An' you know what ol' Rip Ford done said?" John B. Loudermilk asked in his rhetorical fashion. "He done praised young Shapley P. Ross to the skies fer leadin' them Reserve Injuns so good, an' then he done paid tribute to Pitts, Burleson, Nelson an' Tankersley—the men what led his four Ranger detachments.''

He took off his ten-gallon hat and scratched his head. "Now, what was it he said? . . . Oh, yeah," he recalled, putting back his hat. "Ol' Rip said," he paused to clear his throat.

" 'They behaved under fire,' " he continued in a ringing, magisterial voice, " 'in a gallant and soldier-like manner, and I think they have fully vindicated their right to be recognized as Texas Rangers of the old stamp!' "

"Yep, that's jus' what we was—Texas Rangers of the ol' stamp," T.C. Pritchett said loudly, his voice trembling with emotion. "An' by Gawd, we will be agin', one day.''

"You can bet yer boots an' saddles on that," John B. Loudermilk agreed. Then he broke into a wide, boyish grin. "Know what ol' Cap'n Nelson done said 'bout the Rangers?" he asked, pausing to wipe his nose on his fringed sleeve once more.

"He said in his report," the big man with the sandy handlebar mustache went on, " 'The only distinction in the ardor of the entire command was the relative speed of their horses.' "

"Guess that took care of the Comanches for a spell," the Kansan opined.

"Oh, I reckon it did that," Loudermilk agreed. "They done had enuff of us fer some time to come. We taught 'em a lesson, jus' like we done taught one to the Mexicans afore 'em."

"Shore 'nuff," seconded T.C. Pritchett. "Tell 'em 'bout the Mexican War, John. Tell 'em what the Texas Rangers done to ol' Santy Anna an' his boys."

"I'll tell 'em 'bout that over biscuits an' beans," the brawny man told his partner. "For if'n I don't git some food inside me, I swear I'll topple out'n my saddle. Ain't nobody else hungry?" he asked.

They were all hungry; each man nodded his head by way of reply.

"Well, then," John B. Loudermilk said, pulling on the reins and leading his horse off the trail and over to a clump of brush, "git out the skillet an' the coffee pot, an' once't we's filled our bellies, I'll tell ya 'bout the great deeds the Texas Rangers done in the Mexican War."

"Rangers has allus been tough *hombres,*" John B. Loudermilk told Davy Watson and Soaring Hawk, as he spooned the last of his pinto beans out

111

of the battered and dented tin plate he held with his big left hand.

"Guardin' frontiers big as the ones we had in the early days of the Republic calls fer a breed of men what can ride like the wind, scout like an Injun, an fight like a bear what almost lost its balls in a steel trap."

The Kansan smiled as he stretched his arms; then he yawned and leaned back against his saddle, basking in the warmth of the campfire.

Soaring Hawk sat beside him, cleaning his Sharps rifle as he listened and stared inscrutably at the former Texas Ranger.

Somewhere to the north, in the distant hills, a coyote howled at the moon with the voice of a lost soul. The fire flared for a moment, as it consumed dry mesquite, chaparral, and sticks, sputtering and crackling as it cast a bright light on the four men who sat around it. Not far from the campfire, four tethered horses stirred, neighed softly, and switched their tails.

"Rangers got tough from fightin' Injuns an' Mexicans," Loudermilk said as he set his plate down by his side.

"Lots of Injuns," T.C. Pritchett volunteered from across the fire. "Cherokee, Tonkaway, Karankaway, Waco, Tawakoni, an' Comanch'."

"Delaware an' Shawnee was friendly, as was the Tonks later on," added Loudermilk. "But the Comanch' was the baddest Injuns you ever did see. They could ride like devils an' fight like bobcats."

"We done met the Chiricahua Apaches, an' they wasn't no angels their own selves," Davy told him.

The brawny man and his small, sinewy partner

112

both nodded. "They's tough boys, all right," Loudermilk conceded. "But they wasn't as wild as the Comanch'. Why, we still got our hands full with them suckers. Nowadays, they's into cattle rustlin' in a big way."

"Me'n ol' Soaring Hawk learned about that at first hand," the Kansan informed the two men. Then he told them of their capture by Pahanca's Comanches, and their subsequent rescue by Bart Braden.

"You mean the same *hombre* we's about to ride down?" Loudermilk asked incredulously.

Davy nodded. "Those was Bill Fanshaw's cows they run off. An' Bart Braden was Fanshaw's ramrod."

Pritchett stared across the campfire at the Kansan, a puzzled look on his face. "So he done saved your life?"

"I reckon," Davy growled, suddenly looking down as he began to poke among the embers with a stick. "But the sum'bitch gunned me down, later on. An' I sure wouldn't have run into no Comanches in the first place, if'n I hadn't been after him fer runnin' off with that gal, Raquel Mirabal."

"That do make a difference," Pritchett agreed.

"Uh, what was you sayin', Mr. Loudermilk?" Davy asked suddenly, looking up from the embers.

"Oh yeah," rumbled the brawny man with the sandy handlebar mustache. "I was talkin' 'bout how the Rangers got seasoned by fightin' Injuns an' Mexicans. Them Mexicans allus treated us tricky-like. Fust they invited American colonists down into Texas—tha's when ol' Moses Austin an'

113

his boy, Stephen, done come here. An' then, five years later, they tried to kick us out.''

"They tried all sorts of lowdown tricks," added Pritchett.

"They come in an' invaded us a couple of times," Loudermilk told his listeners. "An' they even had them a plot cookin' to raise all the Injuns against us at once't, so that they would jine together an' overrun us Texans. Them Mexes was allus renegin' on their word, an conductin' a heap of treacherous business behind our backs.''

"We done fought the Mexicans fer years," Pritchett said. "An' even defeated ol' Santy Anna at San Jacinto." He sighed. "But they was a heap of Mexicans, an' jus' a handful of Texans.''

"We was plumb lucky that they was havin' a passel of trouble at home in them days," Loudermilk told them. "Or I reckon we'd all be speakin' Spanish right now. They had them two political parties—Centralists and Federalists—what was allus fightin' amongst themselves. And the Frenchies was givin' 'em a hard time, as well. Lucky fer us.''

Pritchett nodded in vigorous agreement.

"Howsomever," Loudermilk went on, "things was still up an' down. We done sent out a ex-pee-dition to Santa Fe once't, hopin' to open up trade, an' we got our butts kicked good fer our pains." He smiled wryly and scratched the stubble on his chin. "We wanted to take the place over by nego-tiation, but the ex-pee-dition warn't well-planned. The Mexes caught our boys an' put 'em in the cala-boose. Hell, they even shot a bunch. The survivors were let go later, an' finally made their way back to

114

Texas.''

"Then the Mexicans come an' captured San Antone,'' T.C. Pritchett informed Davy and Soaring Hawk. "But they done withdrew to the Rio Grande after two days.''

"Later on, they sent this ol' boy—General Woll was his name,'' Loudermilk added, "fer a second surprise attack on San Antone.''

Pritchett chuckled as he recollected those turbulent days. "Me'n ol' John here warn't no more than sixteen or seventeen at the time. We was jus' boys.''

"We mighta been boys, by Gad, but we rid with the Texas Rangers!'' his partner said proudly.

"Yep,'' agreed the other. "An' ol' Jack Hays was leadin' us. He was one of the finest men ever to enter the service.''

"An' ol' Matthew Caldwell,'' Loudermilk said loudly. "He was allus the fust to raise the war-whoop, an' the fust to mix it up with the enemy.''

"Damn straight he was, John!''

"Well, us Texans ree-tali-ated by sendin' our own ex-pee-dition down into Mexico. Onliest problem was that it was full of wild boys and adventurers who wouldn't take no discipline. An' ol' General Somervell jus' had to give it up, 'cause he didn't have him no way of keepin' so many wild galoots in order. So he done headed back up into Texas, takin' 'bout seven hundred-fifty men with him. The remainin' three hundred decided to stay in Mexico an' kick 'em some ass.

"They come to be known as the Mier ex-pee-dition. That was 'cause they started out by attackin' a town by that name. But the Mexican troops arrived in strength, an' the Texas boys had to surrender after a desperate fight, seein' as how they got confused when their leader, William S. Fisher, got hisself wounded. So they surrendered, once't it was agreed they was to be treated as prisoners of war, an' kept near the northern border."

Loudermilk scowed. "But the Mexicans marched 'em over to Matamoros, an' then down to Monterey. It was allus that way," he said bitterly. "You could never trust them greasers no futher than you could toss a Longhorn steer."

"Mexican promises is worth less than Confederate money," commented T.C. Pritchett.

"That's right," said John B. Loudermilk, wiping his nose on the fringed sleeve of his buckskin jacket. "But the boys met up with some other Texans down there, fellas who had been captured at San Antone, an' they all made to escape."

The two Texans exchanged mournful looks.

"They went through the desert, 'twixt Saltillo an' the Rio Grande, an' had the devil's own time of it. They was lost in the desert, without food nor drink, hunted like wolves, an' friend to no man. Purty soon, they was eatin' grasshoppers an' lizards, an' burrowin' in the dry dirt for water, with their tongues all black an' swole. They chucked away their guns to lighten the load. An' some of them got so crazy from thirst that they tried to drink they own pee."

Pritchett shook his head tiredly as Loudermilk went on with his grim narrative.

"Five of 'em died in the desert. Four made it to

Texas. Three was never heard of again. An' all the rest was caught an' sent back to Salado in chains.

"Ol' Santy Anna wanted to have all the Texans shot, but the American an' British ambassadors raised such a ruckus that he only shot eighteen of 'em. The rest was jailed in Mexico City an' Perote prison, where they was treated real bad."

"Real bad," echoed T.C. Pritchett. "Fellas like Big Foot Wallace an' Samuel H. Walker."

"They was finally released, in dribs an' drabs. But there was a lot of hard feelin' 'bout how the Mexicans treated 'em. An' when they come back to Mexico City, at the head of ol' Zachary Taylor's army, them boys done settled more'n a few scores."

"You best believe *that*," Pritchett told Davy and Soaring Hawk.

"They done got even some," allowed Loudermilk.

"Shoot," said Pritchett in a wistful voice, going red in the face as he looked around the campfire. "Them was the days."

"You bet yer boots," agreed his partner. "An' they'll be back again, T.C." He turned to Davy and Soaring Hawk. "Why, we rid with the finest: Colonel Jack Hays, Matthew Caldwell, Big Foot Wallace, William N. Eastland, Samuel H. Walker, and the McCulloch boys—Ben an' Henry."

Pritchett was aroused, now. "Lord, what a sight it was to see Jack Hays mounted on his big ol' bay horse. An' he warn't much more'n a youngster, his own self. No more'n twenty-four or twenty-five. With dark, flashin' eyes, a full head of jet black hair, an' a face plumb full of character. Now, there was a man," he said proudly.

"Did you know," Loudermilk said, pointing to the Kansan's holster, "that yer firearm there was named after a Texas Ranger?"

Davy shook his head as he looked down at the big Walker Colt.

"Shore was," the other continued. "Back in '36, some of the Rangers had got holt of young Samuel Colt's fust revolvers. But they was too dainty, an' nigh onto impossible fer a body to reload on horseback—an' that's what the Texas Rangers needed more'n anything."

"Why, afore the repeatin' revolver was invented, the Rangers had to use single-shot pistols," Pritchett informed Davy and Soaring Hawk. " 'Twarn't like it is nowadays. An' when we done fired all our guns at the enemy, we had to hop down off'n our horses an' charge 'em on foot." He shook his head. "We wasn't no match fer the Injuns, then. Them sum'bitches could send off nine arrows on horseback by the time we reloaded."

"That's the truth," rumbled John B. Loudermilk. "So finally, ol' Sam Walker was sent up to New York, to buy some arms fer the Republic of Texas." He paused to throw some brush and wood on the dying fire.

"Now, ol' Sam was a Injun an' Mexican fighter second to none," he went on, "an' he done tole young Samuel Colt that his new pistols was the best he'd ever come across't, but that they was a mite too light an' flimsy fer reg'lar use on the frontier."

"Y' see, what he needed," interjected Pritchett, "was a pistol what could be loaded in the saddle, whilst an *hombre* was ridin' hell-bent-fer-leather. There warn't no way you could do that with the one he had, 'cause the barrel had to be taken off so's you could replace the empty cylinder with a full one. That meant the rider had to holt onto three parts—tyin' up one hand, whilst he held the rest of the pistol in t'other." He leaned over and spat a gob of tobacco juice into the fire.

"Well now, this made sense to Samuel Colt, an' so he took Sam Walker back with him to his factory in Paterson, New Jersey. An' when ol' Sam finally come back to Texas, he was totin' a batch of new Colts. They was named after him—called the Walker revolver." The wiry Texan squinted as he peered across the campfire at Davy Watson's holster.

"It was a mite differnt from yours, Mister Watson. The fust Walker Colt had a lever rammer attached to the underside of the barrel, which seated the bullets in the chamber without never havin' to remove the cylinder. An' it had more weight an' a perfect balance, so's you could use it as a club to knock out some ornery galoot who warn't wuff shootin'."

Pritchett chuckled. "We bought a few of 'em then, in 1839. But that didn't save young Colt from goin' out of business in 1842."

"Went bankrupt," rumbled Loudermilk.

"When the Mexican War come, we sent ol' Sam Walker back to New York City, for to buy one thousand of the sixshooters from Colt—two fer each Texas Ranger. But Colt didn't hang onto any models, an' Sam didn't bring his with him. Then Colt advertised in the newspapers, but still nothin' turned up. So he designed a new gun fer us—they call it the 'Old Army Type' now. We didn't get 'em in the beginnin', but they did come to Vera Cruz, where we done landed afore marchin' on Mexico City.''

"By Gad, them was the days!" exclaimed John B. Loudermilk, slapping his knee with a meaty hand. "Once't we entered the Union, an American army was headin' by land an' sea to meet the enemy at the Rio Grande, which we claimed as the border with Mexico instead of the Nueces. Well, the U.S. gov'ment was ready to back up its words with action, by gum! 'Cause ol' Zachary Taylor done come down with his boys to kick ass.''

"Ol' Rough 'n Ready," T.C. Pritchett murmured fondly.

"Hot damn!" rumbled Loudermilk, a faraway look in his eyes. "That was the chance't that all us Texans had been waitin' fer—the chance't to fight Mexico on equal terms.'' He rubbed his big, callused hands together and grinned. "We was waitin' a long time fer that little shindig to break out. Why, they was even a song writ to celebrate the occasion.'' The former Ranger began to sing in a rich, rough baritone.

> *"Then mount and away! Give the fleet steed the rein—*
> *The Ranger's at home on the prairies again;*
> *Spur! spur in the chase, dash on to the fight,*
> *Cry vengeance for Texas! and God speed the right."*

"*Eeee-yaaa-a-a-a!*" an excited Pritchett cried at the song's end.

Wide-eyed and caught up in the fervent

memories of the Texans, the Kansan nodded. Even Soaring Hawk leaned forward, watching the two former Rangers with eyes that glittered in the light of the campfire.

"The fustest Rangers to render service to ol' Zachary Taylor was Samuel Walker an' his scouts. Them boys did what the reg'lar U.S. Cavalry couldn't. They went way behind the enemy lines an' sniffed out his whereabouts, then ridin' back like lightnin' to tell ol' Rough 'n Ready—in spite of the fact that the roads was crawlin' with Mexican soldiers."

"Yep," agreed Pritchett. "Fellas without our kind of experience never could've did it."

"What the Rangers done, time an' again, was to git where nobody else could—nor dared," John B. Loudermilk told the Kansan and his Pawnee blood-brother. "Them boys was all ol' Injun an' Mexican fighters from the git-go—cept'n maybe fer some of the East Texas Rangers—an' the best of 'em was in Ben McCulloch's company."

"Yep," Pritchett agreed once more. "Me'n John rid with Ben until the company was disbanded, once't Monterey got took. Then a bunch of the boys went home to look after their families, 'cause the Injuns was a threat on the frontier at that partic'lar time. But me'n John was young an' free, so we jined up with Jack Hays hisself."

"An' we done whipped us some Mexican ass," Loudermilk rumbled warmly. "Both with Jack Hays an' ol' Ben McCulloch."

"Ol' Ben McCulloch," sighed Pritchett. "Why, when we was with him, we was the best-mounted, best-armed, best-equipped an' appointed corps in the rangin' service.''

"An' they was a heap of Rangers in Mexico in them days,'' added Loudermilk. "When it come to danger, Ben McCulloch was the coolest man I ever did see. Why, his face was a mask that would make a Injun's look like a kid making faces through a window pane. An' when a 'mergency come up, it didn't confuse ol' Ben a-tall. Hell now, it jus' quickened his brain. That boy didn't know the meanin' of fear.''

"Damned if'n he didn't,'' seconded Pritchett.

"Ben was a bold 'un,'' Loudermilk told them. "He'd allus struck like a shot—out of the blue—takin' *ranchos* an' villages in his way as he scouted the routes to Monterey. We done traveled more'n two hundred-fifty mile in ten days, trackin' all over enemy territory. We saved the Army a heap of trouble when Ben tole ol' Rough 'n Ready that the direct route to Monterey warn't worth a shit.''

"So we went roun'-abouts,'' said Pritchett, picking up the thread of the story from his partner. "The Texans was fustest, bringing ol' Zachary Taylor with 'em. The Mexicans was all walled up in Monterey, gawkin' out at us an' lobbin' the occasional shot at the troopers. A lot of the soldiers left the ranks an' walked toward the city, hopin' to catch sight of some Mexican soldiers. An' the Texas Rangers rode all around the walls of Monterey on their horses, doin' the tricks they used to do in the old days, when they was in contests with Mexicans an' Comanches.''

"Next day,'' Loudermilk said, "we went down the Marin Road, an' into the chaparral, ol' Ben

McCulloch's boys at the head of the army. We even went under the guns hidden on Independence Hill. We also run smack into a heap of dismounted Mexican cavalry, but we got out an' retired in good order.

"The next mornin', we moved out with Gen'l Worth's boys. An' when we come 'round the *hacienda* of San Jeronimo, we come face to face with a bunch of mounted lancers who was backed up by a lot of infantry. Gen'l Worth gave the order to dismount, but Ben McCulloch didn't receive it. So we met the Mexicans head on an' tore a piece out'n their hides, whilst we cleaned up the Saltillo Road.

"Next, Gen'l Worth decided to take Federation Hill. On one end, facin' us, was a battery of cannon; on t'other, Fort Soldado, which overlooked the city. He sent four artillery companies, which he turned into infantry, up the hill, along with six companies of Texas Rangers—all on foot. The enemy was thick as flies above us, but we soon knocked out the battery. Then we was all tearassin' to the fort, to see who'd get in it fust."

"By jingo, that was a sight!" crowed Pritchett. "All of them boys flyin' over this here ridge—infantry, artillery, the Loo'siana volunteers, an' the Rangers, of course, whoopin' an' hollerin' like Comanches."

"Gad, it was a sight," seconded his partner. "An' a storm was brewin', to boot. Why, the black clouds was so low that the opposin' sides on the heights of Independence an' Federation Hill was firin' cannonballs at each other over the tops of 'em. Soon the storm broke, stoppin' the artillery fire as chain lightnin' struck all over the place an' rain come down in buckets.

"Next day, we went to take Independence Hill. It was three o'clock in the mornin' when we-all went up, but the damn thing was so hard to climb that we was only halfway up by dawn. The Mexicans figgered nobody could git up from the Saltillo Road, an' so they didn't even bother to guard it. Some *did* discover us, as we neared the top, an' they fired off some shots. But none of our boys opened fire 'til we was but twenty yards from the top. Fer a while it was hot an' heavy, but then we done took the hill.

"The final obstacle in our way was the Bishop's Palace. Suddenly, whilst we come up to it, the Mexicans sent up a slew of reinforcements from Monterey, as if they meant to push us off the hill. Quick-like, the Rangers was divided into two companies—Jack Hays on the right, an' Sam Walker on the left. Behind the Rangers was five companies of soldiers. An' in the very front was the Loosiana boys, led by Blanchard." He sniffled and wiped his nose on his sleeve once more.

"Then the Mexicans began to form their ranks afore the palace, with battalions of infantry holdin' rifles what had bayonets fixed to 'em, an' smart-lookin' squadrons of light cavalry with fluttery banners and lances, an' heavy cavalry with fancy helmets an' big swords. Lord, but they was a sight!

"So they began to move toward us, with a rattlin' of swords an' a whinnyin' of horses an' a blowin' of bugles. They made straight fer Blanchard's men, who began to retreat.

"Then we stood up in our cover an' let 'em have it," Loudermilk growled. "Blastin' 'em on the flanks an' in front like a thunderstorm. Then us an' the reg'lar troops all charged at once't, sending the entire Mexican garrison tearin' down the hill like bats out of hell.

"Soon after that, we swept into Monterey, comin' in by two streets what ran parallel. The Mexicans had pulled way back, as far as their Cemetery Plaza, an' it was there that we fust met some stubborn re-sistance."

"Damn straight," muttered Pritchett.

"Had to take them suckers street by street, an' house by house," John B. Loudermilk informed the Kansan and the Pawnee. "They finally had enough after we blowed up an' took their big post office buildin'. After that, the Mexicans wanted to parley." He smiled. "We done whupped 'em good."

"Damn good," seconded Pritchett.

"What happened once't we was in Monterey warn't allus so purty," Loudermilk said. "Y'see, some of the Rangers who had been prisoners thereabouts recognized the fellas what had abused 'em so bad, an' done settled their hash on the spot. It drove the army boys crazy, but there warn't no holdin' the Rangers back."

"They settled a heap of hash, by golly," Pritchett said. "Fer some time after we took Monterey, the soldiers was findin' dead bodies all over the place. 'Cause whenever a Ranger'd spot some varmint who'd tortured an' humiliated him in the old days, why he'd light out after the him, an' shoot that fella down on the spot. An' the next

125

mornin', the soldiers'd find the body."

"Army writ 'em up as suicides," Loudermilk told Davy and Soaring Hawk.

"After ol' Rough 'n Ready broke the back of Santy Anna's army at Buena Vista, they was *guerillas* fightin' all over the place, from Vera Cruz to Mexico City."

T.C. Pritchett giggled. "Them boys *really* drove the Army crazy. So they sent ol' Sam Walker out to fix things up."

Loudermilk began to recite: " 'So *guerillas, robadores,* take warning. . .for the renowned Captain Samuel H. Walker takes no prisoners.' That's what one gent writ."

"He began to clean up right good on the line from Vera Cruz to Mexico City," Pritchett added, growing suddenly grave. "But on the afternoon of October ninth, him an' his boys run smack into Santy Anna an' his full command. The fight was hard an' desperate, an' by the end of it, ol Sam Walker lay dead on the ground, havin' took bullets in the head an' chest.

"That was around the time we-all got our new weapons. All in all, each of us had a rifle, two one-shot pistols, an' a brace of Samuel Colt's new sixshooters. An' we also carried knives, hempen ropes, rawhide riatas an' hair lariats."

"An' by Gad, we was a wild-ass lookin' bunch!" exclaimed Loudermilk, "wearin' long, bushy beards an' long-tailed blue coats, an' bob-tailed black ones, ol' raggedy panama hats, black leather caps an' felt slouch hats. Our horses was all shapes an' sizes an' kinds, from Texas ponies to Kentucky thoroughbreds.

"We was led by Colonel Jack Hays hisself, an' he was jus' the boy to keep the roads open. Once't when we was attacked in a mountain pass by a big force of Mexicans, we emptied all our guns an' then began to fall back, whilst ol' Jack hisself covered our retreat. But purty soon, we got to Mexico City." He cleared his throat, and then spat into the campfire.

"Know what one fella writ about us?" he asked rhetorically. The brawny man began to mimic the speech of an educated Easterner. " 'Hays's Rangers have come, their appearance never to be forgotten. The Mexicans are terribly afraid of them. Today they brought in several prisoners. This is one of the seven wonders. . .for they generally shoot them on the spot where captured.' "

"We shook 'em up when we come into Mexico City, all right," said Pritchett, chuckling as he unrolled his blanket. "They used to crowd the streets when we'd ride by, jus' to get a look at *Los Diablos Tejanos*."

Loudermilk was chuckling now. "That's what they called us: The Texas Devils." He scowled suddenly. "But when we come there, many Americans was bein' killed. So we done give 'em a eye fer a eye, an' a tooth fer a tooth. They also called us *los tejanos sangrientes*—the bloody Texans.

"I'll give you this, we didn't let nobody fool with us. Once't, as we was ridin' by, some sneak thief stole a Ranger's handkerchief. The man what owned it called fer the fella to stop, but the sucker jus' kept on goin'. So the Ranger took out his Colt and put a bullet in 'im. Then he went over to the dead man, picked up his handkerchief, an' went off like nothin' ever happened.'' He shook his head. "Nope, they didn't fool much with the Texas boys."

"Damn, I guess not," muttered the Kansan, shaking his head.

"Once't, when we hit Tehuacan after ridin' all night, we jus' missed ol' Santy Anna hisself. The buzzard must've been warned by spies."

"His apartments was deserted," Pritchett told Davy and Soaring Hawk. "But the table was set fer breakfast, an' candles was still burnin' on it. A crystal inkstand had been knocked over, and the ink was still wet. We jus' missed that sucker."

"Well, we did get a whole lot of goodies he left behind," Loudermilk added. "Santy Anna had a coat what weighed a full fifteen pounds, 'cause it was covered with gold an' decorations. We found lots of Miz Santy Anna's tiny dresses. An' a gold bullion sash, too.

"But the best of all was a cane—made of polished iron, topped by a pedestal of gold tipped with steel. Above that was a eagle chock-full of diamonds, emeralds, sapphires an' rubies—with a diamond in his beak the size of a crab apple."

"It was right purty," Pritchett mumbled as he stifled a yawn.

"We give it to Jack Hayes," Loudermilk told his companions. "But Major William H. Polk seen it, an' hankered to give it to his brother. So Jack give it to him, an' told him to tell President Polk that it was from the Texans."

Davy and Soaring Hawk exchanged wide-eyed looks.

"But we did git to see that ol' sum'bitch, Santy Anna," John B. Loudermilk told them. "When he was leavin' the country, he had stopped at Jalapa. Well, us Rangers got wind of it, an' decided to go there an' gun 'im down when he arrived.

"We was set to kill 'im, for Santy Anna done waged a inhuman an' unchristian war against the people of Texas. Many of us had lost relatives an' friends at the Alamo, Goliad, San Antone, an suchlike places. All we wanted to do was pay the butcher back fer what he done to our people." He shook his head and scowled. "That ain't unreasonable, is it?

"But ol' Rip Ford, Jack Hays, an' some other officers come up to us at Jalapa, an' appealed to our better natures. But he was a cold-blooded murderer, we said, still fixin' to gun him down like a mad dog. They admitted this was so, but added that the world had already condemned Santy Anna fer his butchery of prisoners, an' that his reputation as a soldier was forever stained." Loudermilk smiled a bitter smile.

"Then they asked if'n we-all would dishonor ourselves by killin' him. But we said he was not a prisoner of war. But they said it was the same—he was travelin' under a safe-conduct, an' so killin' him would be somethin' the world would look upon as a as-sass-i-nation. 'You would dishonor Texas!' they said."

Pritchett interrupted with a long, loud yawn. Then the wiry little man stretched out his arms as he lay down, using his saddle for a pillow.

"Well, that done it," Loudermilk resumed. "We wasn't 'bout to dishonor Texas fer nothin'. But we-all did watch ol' Santy Anna come by in his big, open carriage. All us Texas Rangers stood on both sides of the road, an' looked that coyote square in the eye when he passed.''

The Kansan nodded, fully aware that the two former Texas Rangers had lived in the bosom of history.

''His wife was in the carriage—she was a purty l'il thing who smiled an' nodded as if she was goin' to a state ceremony—an' his daughter, too—she kinda looked like him, poor child. An' I swear that sum'bitch went white in the face when he fust seen us, all of his ol' enemies from Texas. He musta had the thought more'n once't that all of us had purty good cause to fill his carcass full of lead. Ain't that right, T.C.?''

The other man said nothing.

''Howsomever, that dog held hisself erect like a soldier ought—I'll say that much fer him. An' all the Texans jus' stared at him whilst his carriage rolled by, all of 'em cold-eyed an' silent as the grave.''

''Judas Priest, he musta shit his pants,'' Davy exclaimed.

Loudermilk smiled at this. ''Soon after that, the war ended. Then we finally went back to Texas.'' He yawned and stretched his arms out in the air. ''Ah, them was the days, wasn't they, T.C.? T.C.?''

Loudermilk turned to his partner, who lay stretched out on the ground with his hat pulled down over his eyes. The only reply he got from the smaller man was a snore.

In an Austin hotel called the Lone Star, Bart

Braden sat alone at a table in the dining room and drank sourmash bourbon, taking his whiskey in a shot glass. Another shot glass sat on the table, by the empty chair across from the ramrod.

Outside, the moon went behind a bank of clouds, and the dark night made itself felt within, its encroaching gloom suddenly contracting the flickering light of the dining room's kerosene lamps. This oppressive change in ambiance caused the people in the room to hunch their shoulders, narrow their eyes, and regard their neighbors with suspicion.

All except Bart Braden. The Texan sprawled comfortably in his chair, a half-smile on his thin lips as he held the glass of bourbon up to the light and turned it slowly, watching the star-like refractions made by the cut-glass.

The ramrod was pleased with the way things had been going for him. Unaware that Davy Watson, Soaring Hawk, and the two former Texas Rangers were on his trail, he had decided to take his ease in the capital for a day or two. He and Raquel Mirabal had earlier enjoyed a long, leisurely dinner, and the young *chicana* was now asleep in her room, with the door unlocked. . .which was something that Bart Braden had never permitted before.

Since the pair had entered the state of Texas, the ramrod had locked Raquel in her room at night. This he had done as much to keep intruders out as to keep his lovely prisoner in. But she had confronted Braden about this only two hours earlier, when he had escorted her back to the room which adjoined his.

"You are going to go out and lock the door

131

now?'' Raquel had asked.

the Texan nodded. ''Yep. Like I been doin' all along, honey.''

''I want you to leave the door unlocked, so that I may open or close it as I choose,'' Raquel told Bart Braden.

''Well, if'n I do,'' he drawled, ''what's to stop you from slippin' out on me?''

''I give you my word I will not escape from this room tonight, *Señor* Braden.''

As he stared at her, the Texan pushed back his hat and began to scratch his head.

Her dark eyes met his. ''Don't lock the door. It makes me feel trapped.''

''You'll gimme your word?''

''I am a Mirabal,'' Raquel said with quiet pride. ''And my honor is precious to me. My word is my bond.''

The ramrod continued to gaze deeply into her eyes for a long time after she had spoken. ''Your word's good enough fer me,'' he told Don Solomon's daughter.

''*Muchas gracias, Señor Braden*,'' she said, nodding to him as he stood in the doorway of the room.

''You *could* call me Bart,'' he told her quietly.

''Good night, *Señor* Braden,'' were Raquel's last words, before she closed the door on Bart Braden.

Notwithstanding that rebuff, the ramrod considered that he had made great progress. In spite of herself, the young *chicana* was coming around. Braden was as determined as ever to possess Raquel Mirabal. . .but it would be with her consent, and no other way. He had patience; he could wait. He was in his home state, and time, so

132

he thought, was on his side.

Chink. The shrill sound of glass making contact with glass cut through the hubbub of the dining room, followed by a soft, gurgling rush, as Braden poured himself a brimming shot of bourbon. He reached out, picked up the glass, and raised it slowly to his lips, taking pains not to spill any of the liquor.

Then, as the ramrod knocked back the shot in one swig, a man came over to his table. The stranger was tall and lean, with a sallow complexion and dark, deep-set eyes. The trigger of his Colt had been filed down, and he wore his holster low, and tied to his thigh with a rawhide thong. And when Bart Braden looked up, he saw that the man had the eyes of a hangman and a smile as cold as the heart of a glacier.

"Mr. Braden?" the man asked in a voice that sounded like sandpaper in a bass register.

The ramrod nodded, straightening up in his seat as he noted that the man's voice was fully as cold and bleak as his smile.

"What can I do fer ya?" Bart Braden asked softly.

"My name's Dan Cain," the stranger rasped. "An' I got me a matter of some importance to discuss with ya, Mister Braden." He gestured toward the empty chair. "Mind if I sit down?"

Braden gave the lanky, cold-eyed man the once-over. "Be my guest, Mister Cain," he replied, smiling his straight-razor smile as he reached for the bottle of bourbon. "Care to wet yer whistle?"

"Don't mind if'n I do," he said hoarsely, taking off his broad-brimmed leather hat as he sat down in the creaking chair.

133

"Here's mud in yer eye," Braden said, raising his glass aloft, still staring at the stranger.

"Bottoms up," the man replied, just before he knocked back his bourbon.

"Arthur Planken told me you was lookin' fer me," Braden drawled, his eyes on the stranger's face. "How'd you know I was in town?"

The man sniffled, pulled out a soiled, crusty handkerchief, and blew his nose in it. Bart Braden poured another round of drinks as he waited patiently for the man to reply.

"Jim Hawkins done tole us," the cold-eyed man told the ramrod as he wiped his nose with the soiled handkerchief. "An' once't ol' Captain Haggerty heerd you was in these parts, he sent me a-ridin' *pronto* to see ya."

Even though his features remained devoid of any expression, Bart Braden's eyes widened at the mention of the name Captain Haggerty.

The man in question, Captain Daniel Patrick Haggerty, was a former officer in the Confederate Army, attached to Baylor's command during the brief period at the opening of the Civil War when the Confederacy had held Texas. Ruthless in enforcing Baylor's own brutal policy toward the Indians of Texas, Captain Haggerty was equally ruthless toward the Union soldiers who became Baylor's prisoners of war. Few of the prisoners in his care survived, but those who lived to tell the tale of the many atrocities committed on the captain's orders caused the Union Army to put a price on the man's head and thereafter try him *in absentia* and subsequently sentence Haggerty to death by hanging.

When the tide of battle turned, and Texas fell to

the Union forces, causing Baylor to beat a hasty retreat, Haggerty and several of his followers—all desperadoes of similar temperament—rode across the Rio Grande, and into the sanctuary of the wild Mexican borderlands. There they mingled with their brother fugitives—renegade Indians, Mexican *bandidos* and revolutionaries, runaway slaves, and deserters from both the Union and Confederate armies. In that no man's land there were outlaws of every stripe: *Anglo* and *chicano*, black and Indian.

Haggerty was now one of the chief cattle rustlers in the southern and eastern parts of Texas. More than a dozen men rode behind him, and the captain often hired out this private army. His allegiance went invariably to the highest bidder. Nor was the man above hiring out his "lads" (as he called them) for various other services of a criminal nature, such as robbery, extortion, and even assassination.

Throughout Texas, New Mexico, Arizona, and northern Mexico, he was known as "Horrible Haggerty," and his men were known by the name of "Haggerty's Hellions." All of the captain's retainers were fugitives of one sort or another, including the remaining Confederate deserters who had originally gone south with him; and those few among them who had not yet killed a man were only waiting for their chance to do so.

To a man, these desperadoes feared and respected Haggerty, for the genial, beefy, red-faced Irishman had put more than a dozen men under six feet of earth. . .and did so each time with a smile on his face. A renegade Catholic, Daniel Patrick Haggerty feared neither man nor God, and firmly believed that the only reward a man enjoyed was in this life, consisting of whatever he could grasp with his own two hands, obtained by way of his own native cunning and ferocity.

Few men in the West were more cunning or ferocious than the sly Captain Haggerty, and few men dared go up against him. He killed without mercy or compunction. The Texas State Police had proved ineffectual in their attempts to bring the outlaw chief to justice, and since the Texas Rangers were no longer in existence, Haggerty felt free to scour the Lone Star State.

"Cap'n'd like to talk with ya, Braden," the tall, sallow man named Dan Cain went on, interrupting the ramrod's thoughts.

"To the captain," Braden said, hoisting his glass aloft and smiling a smile as sharp as the edge of a scalping knife.

"I'll drink to that," Cain replied, hoisting his own bourbon.

"Now, jus' what does the captain want with me, Mister Cain?" Braden asked. "Me'n him ain't 'zactly what you'd call close friends. He done run off some of ol' Bill Fanshaw's cows once't, an' I followed 'im clear into Mexico, an' brought most of 'em back. The captain rode off leavin' five of his boys dead on the ground. An' I caint swear to it, but I think I winged ol' Captain Haggerty, too." Recalling this, the ramrod began to chuckle.

"Yep. You shore 'nuf did," Cain told him, grinning as he scratched the salt-and-pepper stubble on his chin. "You done trimmed off a hunk of the fat what hangs over the captain's belt. Didn't do 'im any real damage, but he was a-cussin' ya fer days—ever' time he done went to stuff his shirt in his pants."

"I was shootin' a mite low that day," Braden drawled. "Lucky thing fer ol' Haggerty, else't I would've put a bullet through his big fat heart."

The outlaw nodded. "We all has days like that, I reckon."

"What's Haggerty want, Cain?" Braden asked once more.

The man squinted at him and leaned across the table, speaking in a low, hoarse voice.

"Don't y'all know what's a-goin' on these days, Braden?" he asked, looking suspiciously around the room.

"I don't catch yer meanin'," the ramrod answered.

"Bill Fanshaw's dead."

"I figgered that, Cain. What else is new?"

"That fella you done shot in San Antone—"

"Sweinhardt?" the ramrod asked contemptuously. "Sum'bitch needed shootin'."

Cain shook his head. "Uh-uh. T'other one. 'Pears he was State Po-lice."

"That ain't no big deal," Braden said, yawning and stretching his arms out in the air. "State Police don't worry me none."

"It's more'n that, Braden," Cain told him. "Turns out he was a ol' Texas Ranger."

Braden shot him a hard look. "So?" he asked, his eyes suddenly narrowing.

" 'Pears that two of his buddies is a-comin' after ya. They was Rangers with him; now they's State Po-lice. They's a-ridin' to git you, Braden. An' they got two more *hombres* with 'em."

The ramrod's eyes widened. "Two more, huh? Who might these fellas be?"

Cain leaned back in his creaking chair. "Don't

rightly know. They got the look of strangers. Heerd they come down from New Mexico. One of 'em's a Injun. Dunno what tribe. Ain't one of our'n.''

"Well, I'll be hornswoggled," Braden whispered, causing the pale, gaunt man to lean in toward him even farther.

"What is it, Braden?"

"Fella with the Injun," Braden said, "he 'bout six-foot tall, with dark blond hair an' blue eyes?"

Cain nodded. "That's him. Says you done shot 'im, an' he owes ya a bullet.''

It was the ramrod's turn to nod. "Yep. I reckon so. But it looks like that sum'bitch was even luckier than ol' Haggerty. We had us a li'l shootout up New Mexico way. That fella done winged me in the shoulder, an I left him fer dead." Braden frowned and shook his head at the thought of his rival for the affections of Raquel Mirabal. "How d'ya like them apples?" he muttered harshly. "Guess I'm gon' have to go out an' kill that sum'bitch all over again.''

"Once't the word of the shootin' of that ol' Ranger gits here in Austin," Cain told him, "they's gonna be a heap of folks out a-lookin' fer ya, Braden. 'Specially since you got that filly with ya.''

Braden's smile disappeared when Cain mentioned Raquel Mirabal.

"Yer a fugitive from the law, yer own self," Cain went on, an evil smirk on his face. "An' so the Cap'n sent me to ask if you could see yer way to lettin' bygones be bygones. He wants ya to throw in with 'im, Braden. Cap'n Haggerty, he got a lot of respect fer a man like you, an' he tole me to tell ya that as sure as God made little green apples, he'll make it well worth yer while.''

Chink. Gurgle. Braden poured two more shots of sourmash bourbon. He was suddenly and painfully aware that his fortunes had taken a sharp turn for the worse, and had begun to weigh the advantages and disadvantages of an alliance with the notorious Captain Haggerty.

''To yer future, Braden,'' Cain rasped as he hoisted his shot glass.

The ramrod shot him a hard look as he knocked back his drink.

''Well, what's it gon' be?'' the outlaw asked, as Bart Braden suddenly rose to his feet.

''Lemme sleep on it,'' Braden told him. ''Where can I find you, Cain?''

''I'm over to Cogswell's place,'' the pale, gaunt man said as he stood up and held out his hand to Braden.

The ramrod shook his hand. ''I'll let ya know in the mornin','' he told the cold-eyed outlaw.

''I'll be waitin','' Cain said as Braden turned and walked off.

The moon had come out again, and its cold light silvered the streets of Austin. The ramrod frowned as he walked in the moonlight, uncomfortably aware that he must make an important decision by morning.

When he finally went to bed, Bart Braden was glum and agitated. It would have cheered the Texan considerably had he known that, by morning, he would once again have the Kansan in his gunsight.

5

Braden and Raquel

Davy Watson, Soaring Hawk, T.C. Pritchett and John B. Loudermilk rode into Austin about an hour after the sun had come up. They took their horses to a livery stable, left them there, and then set out on foot through the dusty streets of the Texan capital, in search of breakfast.

"Pretty place, ain't it?" the Kansan said as he looked at the creamy limestone of the Capitol building glowing softly in the early light. Rolling hills surrounded Austin, and wooded slopes led out to the prairie beyond. Past the Governor's mansion, Davy saw a small church with a fetching German turret; and as he turned his head, he saw a stone church which was considerably larger than the first.

"Austin's s'posed to be bang in the center of the state," T.C. Pritchett informed him.

"Aw, who gives a shit about that, T.C.?" the small, wiry ex-Ranger's partner remonstrated.

"Well, John, not many folks knows that," the shy Pritchett mumbled, going red in the face.

"I surely hope not," Loudermilk growled back.

"Why'd they put it in the center of the state?" asked Davy Watson, his curiosity aroused by now.

" 'Cause they's a bunch of addled ninnies,'' the brawny ex-Ranger muttered darkly. "Who in the Sam Hill gives a damn 'bout why the capital has been plunked down in the 'zact middle of the damn state?''

T.C. Pritchett looked at Davy, and rolled his eyes heavenward.

"They does dumb things like that,'' Loudermilk continued, " 'cause they wants the credit of bein' the first state to plunk its capital smack dab in the middle.'' He scowled and shook his head. "Folks in this country goes hog-wild 'bout breakin' records. An' it don't matter a-tall what the record is. It don't have to be important, nor count fer much. Just so long's the old record has been broke.'' He shook his head again. "Dumbest dang thing I ever heerd of in my whole life.''

"There,'' Soaring Hawk said loudly, causing the three men with him to turn and look where he was pointing.

Hoffmeister's Restaurant, a sign proclaimed above windows distinguished by both their sparkle and the clean white curtains behind them. Outside the place, the boards of the street were still damp from having been recently scrubbed.

Davy sniffed and made out the inviting aroma of homefried potatoes and sizzling bacon. He sniffed again, and picked up the dark, heady scent of freshly brewed coffee.

"Go eat there,'' the Pawnee urged, nodding toward the place.

John D. Loudermilk sniffed loudly. "Damn!'' he exclaimed. "If'n I ever meet up with a lady what cooks stuff that smells jus' half as good as that, by

Gad, I'll marry 'er on the spot."

"Anythin' smells that good caint be bad, John," T.C. Pritchett told his friend.

"How 'bout you, Mister Watson?" Loudermilk asked, turning to the Kansan.

Davy nodded as he spoke. "Why don't we jus' mosey in there, an' take a chance on the place?"

The brawny, mustachioed man nodded in agreement. "Yep. Let's go, fellas. Why, I'm so damn hungry, I could eat a Mexican—sombrero, spurs an' all."

They went up to the door, found the place open, and trooped in. Within ten minutes' time, they were all eating a hearty breakfast of bacon, scrambled eggs, flapjacks, corn pone, home-fried potatoes and coffee.

Hoffmeister was a beefy, bald-headed old German who had been in Texas for more than twenty years. The meal was served by his nephew, a tall, blond young man whose name was Seibert Thurnhofer.

"How long you been here, Zeeburt?" John B. Loudermilk asked the young German.

"Here I am now almost ten months," Siebert replied as he came to the table bearing a second pot of Hoffmeister's delicious coffee.

"Are ya glad ya came to Texas?" Loudermilk asked, continuing his friendly interrogation.

"*Ach, ja*!" Siebert exclaimed. "It iss better a t'ousand time to be in ziss country here."

"Surely things ain't as comfortable here as they was in the Ol' Country?" Davy Watson asked.

"*Was ist dies* com-for-r-r-table?" a puzzled Siebert called out to his uncle, who was already cleaning the grill where he had just been cooking.

"*Gemütlich*," was the old man's reply.

"*Ach, gemütlich.*" Siebert nodded. "*Gemütlich.*" He turned back to Davy. "No. Here is none zo com-for-r-r-table as in Germany. But I like here be-causs I am free."

"You mean you wasn't free back home?" Loudermilk asked Siebert.

The young German shook his head. "There gives no freedom in Germany. The Kaiser rules by the soldier. Zey was to have me in the army, but I come here. I run from zem and come wit Uncle Ludi."

"What d'ya do fer fun, hereabouts?" John B. Loudermilk asked.

"Here it iss hard for the young man to have the fun. Here the *Amerikanisches* gentlemen do not know of the pleasure. When they come for to be *miteinander*. . . ." He looked to his uncle.

"Togedder," Ludwig Hoffmeister told his nephew.

"Togedder," Siebert Thurnhofer repeated. "When ze Texas menfolk comes togedder, all zey do is to drink viskey, play ze cards, and shpit in ze fire."

Davy Watson began to laugh.

"Or zey make ze great row an' punch in ze face each other," Siebert went on. "Or shoot to pieces ze vindows. Ze pleasure here iss not ze pleasure ze gentlemen hass in *Europa*."

"No, it sure as hell ain't, I reckon," the Kansan agreed when he had finally stopped laughing. The two Texans beside him stared at Davy Watson with poker faces.

"He jus' don't unnerstan' local customs," John

B. Loudermilk told Davy, after Siebert had gone back into the kitchen. "From what he done described, I'd say them Texas boys was a-havin' themselves a high ol' time."

T.C. Pritchett nodded as he wiped his chin with a linen napkin. "Them Germans don't know how to have a good time," he said, the expression on his face now as grave as Soaring Hawk's.

"What was you laughin' at before, Mister Watson?" John B. Loudermilk asked as Davy Watson plunked a silver dollar down on the polished table top.

"Oh, jus' somethin' that occurred to me when ol' Zeeburt was talkin'. T'warn't nothin' you boys could catch holt of."

Still poker-faced, the two Texans nodded.

The sun was shining brightly when the Kansan stepped outside Hoffmeister's Restaurant. . .and into Bart Braden's gunsight.

It so happened that Hoffmeister's Restaurant was situated diagonally across the street from the Lone Star Hotel, the place where Bart Braden and Raquel Mirabal were staying. And as the Kansan walked out into the street, it was by a curious coincidence that the Texas ramrod was at one of the windows which faced the restaurant.

He immediately recognized Davy Watson and Soaring Hawk, who followed the Kansan out onto the street. An instant later, Braden had raised the window and was in the process of lining Davy up in his gunsight.

Braden had entered the room only a few

moments earlier, bearing Raquel's breakfast on a tray, as was his custom each morning. After having put the tray down on a night table, the ramrod paused to arrange the flowers which sat on the table in a China vase, flowers he had personally sent up to the beautiful *chicana*.

Having rearranged the flowers to his satisfaction, Braden looked up and gazed idly out the window, his eye suddenly caught by a mangy stray dog that sauntered down the middle of the street.

The dog made its way past Hoffmeister's just as Davy Watson opened the restaurant's front door and came out onto the street. Braden's eyes narrowed as this happened, his glance traveling from the dog to the open door.

"Hey," he murmured in a low voice as he recognized the Kansan. The sound of an opening window was followed by the creak of leather which accompanied the drawing of the ramrod's gun.

"Well, well, well," Bart Braden muttered, his gunsight coming to rest on a line with Davy Watson's chest. "Ain't it a small world," the ramrod told himself, his finger tightening on the trigger of his gun.

"Bart," Raquel Mirabal whispered behind him. "He's not dead—Dah-veed is not dead!"

Braden shook his head, his eyes never leaving the Kansan's form. His eyebrows went up, and a deep crease appeared in his forehead. *It was the first time that she had called him by his name*!

"He's not dead," the young *chicana* whispered. "You didn't kill him!"

Braden shook his head again, his eyes and gunsight glued to Davy Watson. "I reckon not," he whispered back. "Watson's a lucky fella. . . .But his luck done run out." The Texan's finger tightened on the trigger once more.

"No, Bart," Raquel Mirabal whispered urgently. "Don't kill him—please!"

Unseen by Don Solomon's daughter, the Texan scowled. He continued to squeeze the trigger as he moved his gunhand slightly to cover Davy Watson, when the latter stepped off the boards of the sidewalk and into the street.

"He tried to kill me, Raquel," the ramrod said in a husky voice. "An' we done shot it out, fair 'n square. But now he's a-comin' after me at the head of a posse. That's what I done learned last night. So he's fair game, now."

"Please, Bart," she pleaded, "no more killing. There's been more than enough of that already."

There was no emotion in his voice when he replied. "What if I don't shoot hin, Raquel? What then?"

"Bart, I. . ." she began.

"What you gon' do then—ride off with that saddle tramp?" he interrupted, his voice colored by tones of intense bitterness. "I know you was sweet on him, Raquel. That why you want me to spare him?"

"But you *didn't* kill him, Bart," she whispered urgently. "I didn't know that."

"So what?" he said coldly.

"That changes things, Bart," she told the ramrod.

For several moments after she said this, there was silence in the room. Finally, Braden spoke.

146

"What d'ya mean, 'this changes things'?" he asked in a quiet voice.

"Between you and me," she told him. "That's what's changed."

His back still to Raquel Mirabal, the Texan closed his eyes and bit his lip.

"Don't shoot him, Bart," she pleaded again.

"No, I won't, honey," he said with a sigh, lowering his gun as he did.

"Thank you, Bart."

Again there was a long silence, broken only by the creak of leather as the ramrod holstered his gun.

"You fixin' to go to him?" Bart Braden asked in a voice that was barely audible in the room.

Raquel Mirabal stared at the Texan's broad back.

"No," she whispered. "Let *Señor* Watson and *El Indio* ride off. It is enough that you have spared their lives."

Braden's big hands hung by his sides; he began to clench and unclench his fists.

He cleared his throat before he spoke again. "Well, I guess that's the end of the trail fer us."

Raquel's eyes widened. "What do you mean?"

"Yer free to go back yer daddy," he croaked. "I ain't gonna hold you agin yer will no more."

"You would let me go free?" the lovely young woman asked incredulously.

Still looking out the window at the man who had once taken Raquel Mirabal away from him, Bart Braden nodded his head.

"But this changes things, Bart."

Finally the ramrod turned to face her, just as

Davy Watson and his three companions began to walk down the street. A horsefly came in through the open window, and buzzed loudly as its wings rubbed against the glass of the windowpane.

"How does it change things, Raquel?"

"Now I see that you are a man of honor, that you are not a *pistolero*. . .and not a killer."

"I could take Watson in a fair fight any time," Braden told her quietly.

"You are a very brave *caballero, Señor* Braden," Raquel told him, a half-smile upon her lips.

"What you gon' do now?" he asked in a husky voice.

"That depends upon you, *Señor* Braden," she told him, a mischievous gleam coming into her eye.

"I don't catch yer meanin'," he said. "What do ya want me to do?"

She began to move toward him. "I want you to get to know me better. . .Bart."

"Take off yer badge, T.C.," John B. Loudermilk told his partner. "If'n folks knows us fer State Po-lice, ain't nobody gon' tell us a damn thing."

"Reckon you got yerself a point there, John," Pritchett replied, reaching up and unpinning his badge.

"State Police is kinda unpopular, hah?" Davy asked.

"You ain't a-shittin'," the big, brawny man told him. "Ever'body hates or fears 'em. Ain't nobody in the whole damn state what likes 'em."

" 'Cept'n other like-minded varmints an' outlaws," Pritchett added.

"Oh, they ain't all crooked," Loudermilk explained. "They's some good 'uns—honest men like me an' ol' T.C. here. But fer all the good it does, they might as well be crooks. 'Cause the scoundrels is in charge—right up to Governor Davis, the man who done organized the State Police to keep him an' his carpetbag administration in office."

"Reckon that there scalawag's 'bout the biggest scoundrel of 'em all," Pritchett told Davy.

"Ain't a-tall like you said the Rangers was," the Kansan observed.

"Hell, no!" Loudermilk bellowed. "By Gad, there ain't never been nothin' on the face of this earth like the Texas Rangers—nor will there be, I 'spect."

"Y'know somethin', John," T.C. Pritchett told his partner. "We's honest fellas, ain't we now?"

"Damn right we are," the brawny ex-Ranger answered loudly.

"Well, then, I think we's jus' a mite too good fer the State Po-lice." He stared at the badge in his hand for a moment, and then casually tossed it over his shoulder.

"Ain't he somethin'?" John B. Loudermilk said proudly. "Ol' T.C.'s a great one fer doin' the right thing." He unpinned his own badge. "An' I'm right behind ya, as usual, ol' buddy." Then he proceeded to bend the badge double in his thick fingers before throwing it away.

"Le's go an' telegraph headquarters that we

done ree-signed,'' Pritchett told his partner.

"An' then,'' Davy Watson added, "we can finish trackin' down that sum'bitch, Bart Braden.''

Bright and warm, the morning sun streamed through the window of the hotel room, and this time, as Bart Braden made love in a sunlit bed, it was not to some phantom of his imagination. No, this time the Texas ramrod had achieved the fulfillment of his desire: Raquel Mirabal lay naked and willing in his arms, making husky cat-sounds deep in her throat as she urged the man she had once hated on to greater heights of passion and endeavor.

Raquel was making love for what was only the second time in her life, but she took to it as a duck takes to water. And Bart Braden, a man possessed of a fair degree of bedroom expertise, had never been gentler or more adept in his life.

The young *chicana's* head tossed from side to side, her jet-black hair lashing the white pillow, and she closed her eyes and began to moan through clenched teeth.

Bart Braden's hands were caressing her full, firm breasts. His fingers were active, too, as he rolled her thick, erect nipples between thumb and forefinger from time to time, or traced a series of teasing, concentric circles around her large, dark areolae with his fingernails, causing the flesh on her breasts to rise in goose bumps.

"*Ay*,'' she moaned. "*Ay, querido*.'' Suddenly she arched her back, gasped and shuddered. Then, as she relaxed her muscles, Raquel reached down

150

her hands and tangled her long, tapered fingers in the ramrod's curly brown hair.

Bart Braden's face was buried in Raquel's thick muff, and his tongue darted between her nether lips, running up and down their slick pink insides, pausing every now and then to circle and lick the bulb of her clitoris. This elicited a gasp from the New Mexican beauty and caused her to move her pelvis toward him, thrusting her black, silky pelt into his face.

"Oh, Bart," Don Solomon Mirabal's daughter moaned as she writhed beneath the *tejano* enemy of her people. "I feel as if I'm going to explode."

The Texan's only reply was an ardent, rumbling grunt, as he raked the smooth insides of her long, trim thighs with his fingernails and then riffled their sweat-gleaming hollows with his thumbs. After that, he drew his big thumbs down along the outside of the *chicana's* dark, swollen lips.

"*Ay, Dios,*" Raquel moaned as she writhed and thrashed on the bright, sunlit bed, calling her Hispanic God at the onset of ecstasy.

"Oh, Bart. It's rising in me like the Gila River in a flash flood," she moaned, her eyes rolling up in their sockets. "I'm going to—ooooh!"

As she came, Raquel Mirabal lost the power of articulate speech. Her words were suddenly transformed into feline moans and the deep guttural sounds of the puma that ranges the foothills of the Guadalupe Mountains.

Bart Braden's ardent lips and darting tongue had done their work in much the same manner that a flash flood erodes the red-clay soil of northwestern Texas. The Texan's expert and persistent kissing,

151

sucking, licking and nibbling had flooded the *chicana's* nervous system and eroded her consciousness with its resultant orgasmic rush, bringing Raquel, in her dark ecstasy, almost to the brink of oblivion.

"*Dios mio!*" the lovely eighteen-year-old groaned, her tense body suddenly jerking as it began to relax. Her full-lipped mouth hung open, and when Braden came up to kiss it, he found those lips cold with the coldness that succeeds the dissipation of the heat of passion. A red flush had broken out on her cheeks and upon the skin above her breast bone, and she moved her head back and forth slowly upon the white pillow, her eyes closed, sighing like the soft summer breeze which comes down to the prairie from the mountains.

She lay still for a long time, savoring the after-taste of the pleasure which had come to her as a result of her second coupling with a man. And as Bart Braden's big, rough hand began to caress her hair and cheek with a tenderness worthy of the gallant and devoted heroes of medieval European literature, the raven-haired young beauty smiled.

Things had changed for Raquel, there was no doubt about that. Bart Braden was no longer seen by her as a cold-blooded murderer; he was not the *asesino tejano* that she had first taken him for. By this time, her romantic schoolgirl's imagination had made of the rough cowpoke a champion equal in stature to the legendary heroes of the Old World, to Charlemagne's Roland, to the Black Prince, or even El Cid himself, Roderigo Diaz de Bivar, the great knight who gave his life to liberate Valencia from the Moors.

When she opened her eyes again, the first thing that Raquel Mirabal saw was the handsome and square-jawed face of her champion. As he smiled down at her, the corners of his eyes crinkled, and he displayed two rows of white, even teeth.

Raquel's heart opened, and two small tears formed in the corners of her eyes as she smiled back at her Texan lover.

"You all right, honey?" Braden asked with concern when he saw her tears.

"*Si*," she whispered, reaching out her hand and grazing his thin lips with fingers whose touch was as light as the brush of butterfly wings. "Everything is fine, Bart. *Gracias, mi amor. Muchas gracias.*"

There was a strange new warmth in the ramrod's eyes as he gazed down at his love.

"I aim to please you, honey," he whispered back. "More'n anything else."

She stroked his thick sideburns and smiled up at him. "You please me very much," she told him in a husky voice. "And now it is my turn to please you."

Her hand traveled down to stroke the ramrod's hairy chest.

"I hope that I shall please you," Raquel went on. "You must teach me how to please you, Bart, darling."

As she said this, her hand traveled down the Texan's chest, her long fingernails lightly raking his flesh and leaving swaths of goose bumps in their wake.

"You please me plenty all ready, Raquel," Braden told her, in a voice infused with desire and tenderness.

Her hand had descended into the hollow beneath his ribs, and was still heading south.

"I want to please you even more, Bart," she told him, her gaze meeting his as her hand traveled down his belly.

"Ain't nothin' could please me more'n givin' you pleasure, honey," the ramrod told her, his voice now charged with emotion.

"But there is more, *mi corazón*," she whispered, her voice rising like a hot wind from the Mexican interior. "There is more."

Braden emitted an audible gasp as the young *chicana's* long, tapering fingers wrapped themselves around the shaft of his sex, the sudden access of warmth and pressure taking the Texan's breath away.

As she felt the ramrod's cock stiffen in her hand, Raquel Mirabal smiled a bright smile at her lover.

"*Pasión*," she murmured, after licking her full lips. "*Mi pasión es para ti, querido Bartolomeo.*"

"*Pasión*, hah?" the ramrod grunted, smiling a wry smile as he raised his body, feeling the brush of Raquel's thighs beneath him as she parted her legs.

"*Si mi corazón,*" she whispered intensely, guiding his stiff, swollen organ into the dark and scented grotto of delight between her long, trim thighs,

"*Ay-y-y-y*," she gasped as the Texan entered her with a squish. And Bart Braden gasped too, as he felt the tight, intimate grip of the beautiful eighteen-year-old's warm, wet pussy.

"Oh, Bart," Raquel whispered intensely, as her lover began to stroke, slowly and deeply, causing the young *chicana's* pelvis to twitch in anticipation and the muscles in her abdomen to contract.

Braden was smiling through clenched teeth as he slid his throbbing cock deeper into the hot, welcoming sheath of his beloved, the woman for whom he had started a range war and surmounted all obstacles in the path of his desire, his dark angel of passion.

"*Te quiero mucho*," he grunted, declaring his desire in Raquel's native tongue.

Her eyes were glazed and she writhed beneath him, as heat and pressure spread in her groin with the swiftness of a forest fire.

"I want you, too, Bart," she whispered back, just before the welcome, brain-searing blackness and the tidal wave breaking in her groin swamped her consciousness. "I want you very much."

The Texan emitted a sharp, sudden wail, sounding as if he had just been stabbed in the back. His body was seized by a succession of violent tremors, and he called out in the bright, sunlit bedroom with the voice of a man drowning in some vast, dark ocean.

"Oh, yes, Bart. Yesss," Raquel hissed as the serpent of desire uncoiled in her groin and began to thrash about wildly, lashing her on to a sudden and unexpected climax, the Texan's orgasm having greatly excited the young beauty.

They came together then, their groins butted at the crescendo of their passion, Raquel's straight black thatch interwoven with the dark brown pubic curls of her lover. The *chicana's* contralto wails complemented the baritone groans of the Texan.

After the tidal wave of their shared passion had

crested and ebbed, the handsome pair fell into a sleep as deep and dark as the bottom of the far-off Atlantic Ocean, an ocean which neither of the lovers had ever seen. And while they were steeped in the dreamless blackness that follows upon total satiety, the morning sun continued to shine through the window of the hotel room, its light gilding the recumbent forms of Bart Braden and Raquel Mirabal.

6

Captain Haggerty's Hellions

Captain Daniel Patrick Haggerty shifted his two hundred and eighty pounds in the saddle, squinted as he looked off into the sunlit distance, and scratched the copper-colored stubble on his chin, the sound made by his nails running over those bristles resembling the crackle of a distant brush fire.

"Jesus, Mary an' Joseph," the big Irishman swore. "Now, where d'ya suppose that Braden fella could be?"

Beside him, on his left, a tall man with a bald head and a black patch over his left eye replied in a bass voice. He was Eli Satterthwaite, a long-time desperado, and an ex-Texas Ranger, one who had been drummed out of the service after being convicted of rustling and extortion.

"It ain't five o'clock yet, Cap'n," Satterthwaite reminded Haggerty. "If Bart Braden said he'll be here, he'll be here."

The captain reached down his left hand and patted the roll of fat that overflowed the upper edge of his gunbelt, touching the place where Bart Braden had shot him years before.

"D'ya suppose the lad will bring the Mexican

wench with him?" he asked.

This time he was answered by the man on his right, a short, stocky fellow with a bowl haircut and buck teeth. Richard Lingeman was the man's name, and he had been an officer in the Confederate Army, serving under Haggerty during the Civil War. He had fled to Mexico along with his chief, rather than risk a court martial and subsequent firing squad for the many atrocities he had committed on the Irishman's orders.

"If'n he brings the gal, it might be a good thing fer us, Cap'n," Lingeman told Haggerty. "I hear tell she's a purty li'l tamale."

"Heh, heh, heh," chuckled the graybeard behind him. The man sat tall on a black stallion; he must have been at least in his middle sixties, but appeared to be as physically powerful as any of the twelve other bully-boys who rode with Captain Haggerty. He tended to the band's wounds, and his name was Doc Doucette.

"If you dast touch that there little tamale, ol' Bart Braden'll blow yer clinkers off," the old man boomed in a resonant bass voice. "Heh, heh, heh. Ain't you heerd what he done to ol' Ford Sweinhardt in San Antone?"

"Sweinhardt warn't no sickly little fella, neither," chimed in the man beside Doc Doucette. He was a small, skinny, weasel-faced man known as Squint Ryerback. The "daddy" of all cattle rustlers in West Texas, he had spent the last few decades preying on the Longhorn herds there, and in the New Mexico Territory as well.

Richard Lingeman smiled and displayed his maloccluded teeth. " 'Twarn't me Bart Braden done shot," he said with a leer, rolling his eyes in the direction of the tubby, red-faced Captain Haggerty.

Eyes widened to the size of small saucers, and jaws dropped to the end of their hinges when the desperado made this remark.

The beefy Irishman shook his head as he turned to Lingeman. "Bedad, it's a forward fella y'are, Dickie," he exclaimed loudly, in reply to the other's thinly veiled reference to his shooting by Bart Braden. But as he said this, Haggerty was smiling paternally at the outlaw.

Lingeman had the distinction of being the captain's favorite, as well as his right-hand man. Had anyone else in the band of ruffians made such a remark, it was dollars to doughnuts that he would be crying out in pain and writhing in the dust a moment later, with two slugs from the Irishman's sevenshooter in his belly.

The captain's smile was taken as permission to laugh, and the remaining eleven outlaws all began to snicker or guffaw at Lingeman's wit.

"Well, well, well," Captain Haggerty said genially as he surveyed his band of cutthroats. "So yez are all amused by Dickie's bright remark, are yez? Well, in that case, Dickie me lad, if Mister Bart Braden ever gets it in his head to quarrel with Haggerty's Hellions, I'll leave it up to you to teach that boy-o some respect."

The bully-boys began to snicker. Lingeman went red in the face as he glared at his fellow outlaws, shooting nasty looks at them, looks that were as hot as a flaming arrow.

"Well," the desperado mumbled, sniffling and

159

patting his dusty holster, "if'n Bart Braden needs a lesson, then I'm just the *hombre* what can teach it to him."

"Deeckie ees no virgin when it come to takin' care of bad *hombres*," a potbellied Mexican named Eufemio Salcedo told the others. "I seen him make *muchas muertes*, many dead men, *amigos*."

Wanted on both sides of the Rio Grande, Salcedo and the man beside him, his brother, Fernando, were notorious cutthroats and expert rustlers who had joined forces with Haggerty years earlier. Their intimate knowledge of the territory south of the Rio Grande was invaluable to the outlaw band.

Lean and handsome where his brother was squat and ugly, Fernando Salcedo nodded empthatically, seconding Eufemio's words.

"*Ach du lieber*!" bellowed a huge, bearded German named Oberst. "Bart Braten iss not zo easy to zhoot. Maybe Tickie zhoult go after him ven he iss azleep."

The desperadoes laughed loudly at this.

Linegeman's eyes narrowed as he took the big German's measure. Oberst was no great shakes with a sidearm, he knew that, but the giant had killed more than half a dozen men with his bare hands.

"You ain't so damn funny—y'know that, Oberst?" Lingeman growled, the fingers of his gun-hand twitching by his holster.

"Ah, now, where's yer sense of humor, Dickie-boy?" Captain Haggerty called out loudly, clapping Lingeman on the back as he did.

"An' youse guys t'ought dat Joymans had no sense of humor, huh?" a burly man with a waxed mustache and thinning brown hair chimed in. His name was Michael Shaughnessy, and he was a tough who hailed from the ferocious New York City slum neighborhood known as Hell's Kitchen. He was a professional assassin, and was used whenever Haggerty had a score to settle.

"Ah say, where's yoah sense o' humor, Richud?" asked a lean and solemn-faced man with black muttonchop whiskers. His name was Arthur Danforth. He was a Virginian by birth, and an outlaw of necessity, having fled prosecution for the crimes he had perpetrated as one of the ranking officers in the notorious Confederate prison at Andersonville, Georgia.

"Ah, c'mon, Dickie-boy. Give us a smile," coaxed Daniel Patrick Haggerty.

"It vas chust a choke," the massive German rumbled, holding out his two carpet-beater hands. He sat astride a big brown gelding, but his huge frame made it look more like an Indian pony.

"G-g-g-give ol' F-f-fritz yer h-hand," stammered a small man with blond, Bill Cody hair, and an Adam's apple the size of a goose egg. He was physically unprepossessing, but was a crack shot whose deadly skill with rifle and pistol had earned him the name, Dead-Eye Dan Bates.

Behind Dead-Eye Dan was another horseman, a huge Indian, who nodded in agreement with the little man's words. His name was Puma, and he was a Jicarilla Apache, one whose viciousness and double-dealing practices had caused his own people to banish him from their campfires.

"Ah, go on, lad," Haggerty urged his favorite. "Give ol' Fritzie yer hand."

"All right," Lingeman grunted, scowling as he slowly extended his hand to the German. "But it warn't funny."

As his huge hand encircled Lingeman's, the German sneered. "You got to learn to take a choke, Tickie," he rumbled.

Feeling the sudden pressure on his gun-hand, Lingeman tried to jerk it back, glaring angrily at the giant as he did. But his hand remained imprisoned within Oberst's massive paw.

"Tut, tut, tut, Fritzie, me bucko," Captain Haggerty cautioned. "None o' yer little parlor games now." He turned in the saddle and looked around at the assortment of desperadoes behind him.

"I want yez all to remember that we're just one big family. Why, just t'ink of me as yer beloved father, boys, as yer dear ol' da'."

The German exploded into laughter at this, and let go of Lingeman's hand. In another moment, he was joined by the other bully-boys. Even Lingeman had to laugh, his discolored buck-teeth jutting out of his mouth as he did.

"Now, that's better, me lads," Haggerty said cheerfully, beaming at his family of cutthroats, bushwhackers and rustlers. "Oi want yez all to get on loike kissin' cousins."

"Cap'n, they's a cloud of dust up ahead," Squint Ryerback called out, pointing westward.

"Man and woman ride with Dan Cain," Puma the Apache told his leader, naming the last remaining member of Haggerty's Hellions, the man

162

whom the captain had sent to palaver with Bart Braden.

"Now, ain't that gratifoiyin'," the beefy Irishman said sweetly. "It looks as if Mister Braden has seen fit to jine us."

"Heh, heh, heh," chuckled old Doc Doucette, as he turned to Richard Lingeman. "This ought to be good, boys. This ought to be good."

The other bully-boys smiled and nodded their heads. All except Richard Lingeman, who narrowed his eyes and began to scowl darkly at the approaching riders, at the tall, broad-shouldered cowboy who rode beside Raquel Mirabal and the desperado known as Dan Cain.

"So he went over to Haggerty, by Gad!" swore John B. Loudermilk, banging his meaty fist down on the bar of the Lone Star Hotel. "Well, how d'ya like them apples, boys?"

"Reckon we-all got our work cut out fer us, John," T.C. Pritchett dead-panned.

"Well, they's sure 'nuff gon' be a heap of fightin'" Loudermilk agreed. "They's 'bout fifteen guns in that gang, countin' that fat ol' scoundrel, Haggerty."

"An' Braden's worth four or five ord'nary men," the Kansan acknowledged grudgingly.

"Bee-jabers!" exclaimed the barkeep, a thin, balding man named Joe Smith. He had overheard Bart Braden's conversation with Dan Cain, and had relayed the information to Pritchett and Loudermilk, both long-time friends of his.

"Yep. 'At's a passel of guns, all right,"

Loudermilk admitted after he had wiped his nose on the sleeve of his fringed buckskin jacket.

"You don't look discouraged any, John," Joe Smith said as he leaned over and began to wipe the bar.

"Not a-tall, Joe," the brawny man replied. "Them's Texas Ranger odds. Me'n ol' T.C. here's used to goin' up agin' that many guns."

Pritchett nodded. "Ain't nothin' new fer us, Joe."

"What about you fellas?" the barkeep asked, looking from Soaring Hawk to the Kansan.

"Ain't nothin' new to us, neither," Davy Watson told the man, recalling the Battle of Beecher's Island and his life-and-death showdown with the Landry Gang in Hell's Canyon.

"Just mean more to kill," Soaring Hawk assured Joe Smith, as the barkeep handed him a second glass of sarsaparilla.

"Well," Smith said to the four men who stood on the other side of the bar, "I 'spect y'all got yer work cut out fer ya."

" 'Member, this here's special," John B. Loudermilk rumbled. "We's got two good reasons to light out after 'em, Joe. First, that Braden fella done gunned down ol' Paul Myers. An' second, we been after that fat sucker, Haggerty, ever since sixty-five."

"This gives us a chance to settle both scores, Joe," T.C. Pritchett told the barkeep.

"Well, y'all take care," Joe smith called out as the four men walked out of the bar and dining room of the Lone Star Hotel.

"Don't you worry none 'bout us, Joseph," John

B. Loudermilk called back over his shoulder. "It's Bart Braden an' that nest of vipers what's got to watch out."

Outside the Lone Star Hotel, the four men mounted their horses and proceeded to ride out of Austin, heading in an easterly direction.

Through the agency of a Mexican named Juan Bedoya, a long-time paid informant of theirs, the two ex-Rangers had learned of Braden and Raquel's departure in the company of Dan Cain, only a few hours earlier.

By the time that the sun was past high noon, the four riders had picked up Braden's trail, and were gaining on him with every passing mile. And by the time that they sat down to supper around a roaring campfire, the Kansan had calculated that they would overtake the fugitives sometime in the latter part of the coming morning.

Captain Daniel Patrick Haggerty's pig-eyes glittered as he stared at the young, raven-haired beauty who rode toward him, flanked by the Texas ramrod, Bart Braden, and the thin, cadaverous-looking desperado, Dan Cain.

The men who surrounded the tubby, red-faced Irishman all stared at the young *chicana* with burning eyes. Although Bart Braden was the eagerly awaited visitor, Haggerty's Hellions had immediately, and to a man, turned their attention to the proud daughter of Don Solomon Mirabal.

Riding at her left hand, the pale outlaw with the black pencil-mustache had a faint, self-satisfied grin on his face. He had brought a new recruit for

Captain Haggerty, a man who had never before been on the wrong side of the law, but who was at the same time one of the toughest and deadliest men in all Texas.

This the desperado considered to be a feather in his cap, for the major gainful employment of Haggerty's Hellions—extortion, thievery and murder notwithstanding—was cattle rustling. And who knew the great Longhorn herds of Texas and New Mexico better than Bart Braden, the top hand who had been for many years foreman and trail boss for Bill Fanshaw, the cattle baron who had lost his life in the recent attack upon the spread of Don Solomon Mirabal?

Captain Haggerty was overjoyed. Having Bart Braden as an ally, the Irishman reckoned, would give him access to the pick of the herds of such renowed cattle barons as John Chisum and Charlie Goodnight, to say nothing of the late Bill Fanshaw's Longhorns, which were grazing peacefully to the north, just begging to be led away, like so many sheep. And make no mistake about it, Daniel Patrick Haggerty firmly believed that he was the shepherd to lead that particular flock to greener pastures.

For his part, Bart Braden appraised Captain Haggerty and his Hellions with a cold eye. Here he was, the ramrod told himself, riding with Raquel Mirabal, the woman he loved, into a den of thieves and murderers. They were fourteen mean and vicious *hombres*—including Haggerty, the cruelest and most cold-blooded of them all. Ordinarily, Braden would not have trusted them any farther than he could have heaved a brahma bull; but as things stood now, the ramrod considered them to be a necessary evil—for the present.

The shooting of a Texas state policeman had made him the object of a statewide manhunt, or so Braden thought once he had learned that the two men who rode with Davy Watson and Soaring Hawk were brother-officers of the dead man. He knew nothing of the fact that the state policemen were riding out after him for personal reasons, or that they had once served as Texas Rangers under the man he had killed.

The presence of state policemen on his trail so soon after the incident in San Antonio led the ramrod to believe that the State Police were indeed scouring the lower half of the Lone Star State for him. Normally this would not have particularly disturbed him, since Braden was a man who could take care of himself in any situation, but this time there was a further consideration and a greater responsibility.

While Bart Braden gave little thought to his own safety, he gave much thought to that of Raquel Mirabal. He had to get her out of Texas, and as soon as possible. And the safest way to achieve this goal, the ramrod had decided, was to form a temporary alliance with Captain Haggerty. But there would be a price for Raquel's safety, he knew that; the devil would have to be given his due. Braden did not know exactly what he was going to do as he rode up to Haggerty and his Hellions; and although he looked confident and determined, the Texan was far from clear as to the best way to get Raquel Mirabal out of Texas.

As for Raquel herself, while aware that she was

in an increasingly dangerous situation, the eighteen-year-old was at the same time thrilled beyond her wildest imaginings.

Her school friends would never believe what was happening to her—not in a thousand years! And if they should, why, each of them would turn green with envy, for Raquel Mirabal's daily life had become the veritable embodiment of the deepest romantic fantasies of the *muchachas* of the convent school of Our Lady of Guadalupe.

In one stroke, through the agency of her abductor, Bart Braden, Raquel Mirabal had found love, romance and adventure. It was a young girl's dream. And now that the Texan had proved himself an honorable man, Don Solomon's daughter gave herself freely to him, immersing herself in a stream of extravagant characters and colorful adventures. And because she felt so secure under the protection of her formidable lover, the young *chicana* consequently ignored the grim reality of her situation.

"Well, well, well, if it ain't Himself," Captain Haggerty called out in a cheerful voice as Braden drew near. "If this ain't a pleasant surprise."

Braden wore a poker-face as he nodded slightly and murmured, "Haggerty," by way of acknowledgement.

"Oh, an' such a lovely lady," the captain cooed. "Prettier flower never grew in the state of Texas. Captain Daniel Patrick Haggerty at yer service, Miss." He took off his dusty hat with a flourish, and bowed as low in the saddle as his great belly would permit.

Enchanted and embarassed at the same time by

the Irishman's gallantry, Raquel Mirabal lowered her eyes and nodded in acknowledgment of the compliment.

Braden's glance traveled over the band of ruffians who sat to horse behind Captain Haggerty. To a man, they looked mean, low-down and dangerous. Not the traveling companions he would have chosen under normal conditions, Haggerty's Hellions were just what he needed to get Raquel and himself out of Texas in one piece.

"We rode out here to meet yez," Haggerty told Braden and Raquel with a smile. "Our camp's back a few moiles, in a noice outta-the-way place. Why don't yez come there, an' break bread with me an' my lads?"

Bart Braden nodded. His eyes were cold and his thin lips were set in a grim, dangerous smile, an expression which had come upon his face when he saw the way that Haggerty's Hellions were eyeing Raquel Mirabal. This annoyed the ramrod, but it did not worry him overmuch. From his earlier talk with Dan Cain, he had gathered that Haggerty and his men had knowledge of the circumstances which had led to the shooting of Ford Sweinhardt, and he felt sure that none of the desperadoes would have the stomach to go up against him, even for a prize such as the beautiful young *chicana*.

They rode off in a northeasterly direction, Braden and Raquel riding with Captain Haggerty, and the rest of the desperadoes following close behind them. Before long, the riders came to a creek, which they followed as it began to meander through several large clusters of boulders. There, in the midst of that natural fortification, they came upon the outlaw camp.

A fire was burning there, and a kettle was simmering above it, tended by a bald-headed Negro mute named Jimmy Blount. He had been Haggerty's manservant since the days before the War between the States, and the Irishman jokingly referred to him as his son.

"Oh, I hope it's somethin' tasty an' fillin' ye've cooked up fer yer auld da'," the captain wheezed as he climbed down from his horse.

Jimmy Blount nodded eagerly, and grunted in reply. His skin was blue-black in color, and when he smiled, his teeth appeared whiter than the keys of a new pianoforte.

The contents of the kettle proved to be an Irish stew, and it was tasty indeed, the riders found out, once they had tended to their mounts and seated themselves around the campfire.

In addition to the stew, Jimmy Blount had baked sourdough biscuits. There was even dessert, in the form of dried fruit. The meal was washed down with steaming cups of the bitter black coffee of the trail.

"I doubt that God in his heaven ever doined any better," Haggerty said, mopping up the last of his gravy with the remains of a sourdough biscuit. "An' if, as I personally t'ink, there ain't nobody up there," he went on, cocking an eye at the heavens, "then we've had the best of it, ain't we?" He sighed and made a declamatory gesture with his hands. "Ah, well, it's eat, drink an' be merry, for on the morrow we shall die."

B-w-w-woarp! Oberst, the German, rent the air with an ear-splitting belch.

"Ah, man, ye've got no respect for foine sentiments," Captain Haggerty complained. "Here I am, expressin' deep an' elevated feelin's, an' what d'you do, Fritzie? You belch loike a hog at a trough. Now, appolly-joize to the young lady, won't ya?"

"*Ach, entschuldigen sie, fraülein*," the giant rumbled in a *basso profundo* as he blushed and bowed to Raquel Mirabal.

"Well, now," Haggerty said, rubbing his pudgy hands together and turning to face Bart Braden. "I t'ink it's toime that we was talkin' about what we moight do fer each other, Mister Braden."

The ramrod met his eye and nodded.

"I'm sure you know what would fill my auld heart wi' cheer," the captain told him. "Gettin' my hands on a few t'ousand head of Texas Longhorn—that's what I'd loike most in all the world, Mister Braden." He had a sly smile on his red, puffy face. "Now, what would you be loikin' most?" he asked the ramrod.

Braden put his hand on Raquel Mirabal's knee. "I want to get this lady an' me outta Texas in one piece," he told the beefy Irishman.

"An' ya want me'n my lads to make sure you get out safe, hah?"

Braden nodded again.

"Well," Haggerty grunted, straightening up and rubbing his hands togerther, "an' what would ya be t'inkin' of doin' fer us in return?"

"How 'bout gittin' you all the Longhorns you can herd south?" was the ramrod's reply.

"Ah, now yer playin' a chune that's sure to set the loikes of Paddy Haggerty an' his boys to jiggin'," the captian told Bart Braden, smiling an avaricious smile as he did.

"I'll see that you git yer fill of Bill Fanshaw's Longhorns," Braden said to Haggerty. "An' I'll show ya the safest way to git 'em out'n the New Mexico Territory."

"Oh, yer just the one to warm an' auld fella's heart," Captain Haggerty cried out in an ecstasy of greed.

"But first, I want yer help in gittin' Miss Mirabal to Loosiana," Braden went on. "We'll drop her off in Shreveport—jus' across the state line. An' then I'll ride back with you an' yer boys, an' lead y'all to the pick of Bill Fanshaw's herds."

Haggerty scratched the stubble on his jowls and sighed. "Now, I'd loike to do that, Mister Braden, really I would. But I'm afraid that I can't."

The ramrod shot him a hard look. "Why the hell not?" he asked.

"Because," the Irishman replied reasonably, "I need the young lady around fer reasons of security. . .to guarantee that you do the job proper-loike, so to speak."

"You sayin' you don't trust me, Haggerty?" the Texan growled.

"Now, now, Mister Braden, I wouldn't say that. It's not the sort of thing you should take personal-loike. Remember, if ya will, that fer a fella loike meself to survive in a line of work such as this one, it ain't a good idee to trust anybody. D'ya see what I mean, now? So let's just consider what I said a condition of our little business transaction, shall we?"

"What about about her?" Braden asked

roughly.

The captain beamed at him. "Oh, ya have no need a-tall to worry about the young lady, I can assure you of that. She'll be safe an' snug while we're out on our little round-up. I promise ya there won't be the sloightest danger to her."

Braden's eyes narrowed as he stared at Captain Haggerty. "Damn well better not be," he growled testily. " 'Cause if so much as a hair on her head is mussed when we git back, Haggerty, I'm gon' hold you personally responsible."

"Why, she'll be as safe an' comfy as if she was in some grand ol' hotel in New York or London," the beefy, red-faced Irishman said, smiling beatifically as he looked from Raquel to Braden. "We'll just roide over to Hodgson, a town not far from here, where a good friend of mine will put up Miss, ah—" Here he stopped to look inquiringly at Raquel.

"Mirabal," she replied, suddenly embarrassed by the outlaw's attentions.

"Miss Mirabal," Haggerty resumed. "Why, my auld pal, Monte Tittiger, an' his woife, Ethel, will see to it that Miss Mirabal gets the best of treatment whoile we're away. An then, when we've concluded our business, Mister Braden, you can drop boi Tittiger's place fer the young lady. An' me an' my lads will be more than deeloighted to escort yez into the fair state of Louisiana."

This was not what Bart Braden had intended to settle for when he first rode into the outlaw camp; but he had shot Haggerty once, and could therefore see the man's point in wishing to retain Raquel Mirabal as a hostage.

The Irishman was no fool, the Texan acknowledged ruefully. And if, as he thought, there was a manhunt on for him, then sticking with the outlaw band until he and his love were out of the state would certainly be the wisest course to follow. Haggerty commanded a small army, and the State Police had proved totally ineffectual in bringing the outlaw and his followers to justice.

It would have been a different story in the days of the Texas Rangers, Braden reminded himself. But there just didn't seem to be any men of that caliber in the ranks of the State Police. . . .

"Well, me friend," the captain said cheerfully, "now, what'll it be? Will ya t'row in wit' us for this one grand round-up? Will ya lead Paddy Haggerty an' his children to the Promised Land? Will ya lead us to Bill Fanshaw's Longhorns?" He smiled sadly at the ramrod. " 'Tis certain that poor Fanshaw—God rest his soul—" here he paused and crossed himself—"will be needin' 'em no longer."

"Oh, yeah," chuckled Richard Lingeman. "All that beef'd jus' bar-be-cue in hell."

When he heard this last remark, Bart Braden stiffened. Then, with trembling hand he tilted back his hat and slowly turned to face the buck-toothed desperado. The ramrod was smiling that dangerous, straight-razor smile of his, and he regarded Lingeman with eyes that were colder than a tombstone in Alaska.

"Bill Fanshaw was my friend, mister," he said quietly, still smiling his grim smile at Richard Lingeman. "An' if I hear you make another stupid remark about him, I'm gonna knock all them

174

snaggle teeth of your'n right down yer throat."

Lingeman's eyes went wide and his jaw dropped at this. Then, after having gasped several times and taken several deep breaths, the outraged bully-boy glared at Bart Braden and growled his reply to the ramrod's threat.

"You mus' be gittin' ready to jine Bill Fanshaw in hell yer own self, Braden," Haggerty's favorite told the Texan in the heat of anger. " 'Cause you done talked that shit of your'n to the wrong *hombre*, this time."

Watching this encounter breathlessly, Raquel Mirabal saw the steely glint in her lover's eye and suddenly became ᴀfraid.

Braden rose slowᴧ to his feet. "Think you're the right man to take me, Bucktooth?" Braden asked in a quiet voice that was as hard as the head of a bullet.

"Now, now, me lads," Captain Haggerty called out, an edge of anxiety to his cheerful and conciliatory tone of voice.

"Keep out of this, Cap'n!" roared a furious Lingeman. "You heerd what he done called me. Nobody calls me that—an' lives!"

"Ah, Dickie-boy," the captain pleaded, "sure, an' the man didn't mean nothin' by it." He turned to Bart Braden, and shot him an imploring look. "Tell 'im you didn't mean nothin' by it, Braden. Now, go ahead, won't ya?"

By this time, Lingeman had jumped to his feet, and all the desperadoes near him backed away, intending not to get caught in the line of fire, should a gunfight occur.

The Texan's eyes glinted like sunlight on a gun

barrel, and his smile was as bleak as a hangman's heart.

"Tell 'im you was only joshin', Braden," Captain Haggerty pleaded, aware that someone would soon be lying dead upon the ground if he could not placate the two hard and violent men who faced each other across the campfire.

Dan Cain, who was near Bart Braden, gently pulled Raquel Mirabal with him as he stepped out of the line of fire.

The ramrod saw this out of the corner of his eye, and nodded to Cain. His cold eyes never left Richard Lingeman, who now stood rocking slowly back and forth, looking ghastly and sinister in the firelight, the fingers of his gun-hand fluttering nervously above his holster, like bumblebees hovering over a daisy.

"Now, for God's sake, man," Captain Haggerty implored the ramrod, "tell auld Dickie ya didn't mean nothin' by what ya said just now." The beads of sweat that streaked the Irishman's face glimmered like diamonds in the dancing light of the outlaw campfire.

As he listened to Haggerty, Braden watched Lingeman with the cold and predatory eyes of a hawk. "What I meant to say," he began, "was that ol' Dickie here. . ." Suddenly he paused, causing all the outlaws to lean toward him and cock their ears in his direction, anxiously awaiting the Texan's next words.

Lingeman's face was red as a beet, as he angrily gaped at Braden, and his eyes looked as if they were about to pop right out of his head.

"Ol' Dickie here," Braden drawled, resuming

after an uncommonly long pause, "is jus' 'bout the ugliest fucker I ever done set eyes on. . .north or south of the Rio Grande."

That did it. Lingeman emitted a scream of rage. His hand darted down to the sixgun at his side.

BLAMBLAM!!

Two shots rang out loudly in the Texas night, splitting the air with their belling roars.

Richard Lingeman shot backward, blown off his feet, and fell down on his back in the dust, his chest and heart blown apart by the two big slugs from Bart Braden's Colt .45.

"Oh, Jesus God—ye've killed him!" screeched Captain Haggerty, wringing his hands as he regarded the bloody bundle of meat and rags that had been Richard Lingeman.

Braden's gun was still smoking when he holstered it. "He made his play an' lost, Haggerty," the ramrod quietly told the devastated Irishman. "Sum'bitch asked fer it."

"Ah, fer the love of Christ," the captain wailed in a voice that quavered and broke, "ye had no cause to kill poor little Dickie over some stupid remark he made."

"I told you before," Bart Braden said quietly, "Bill Fanshaw was my friend."

Raquel Mirabal's wide eyes were gleaming as she looked up at her champion. He had Spanish pride, that one. He had not hesitated to defend his honor against these *bandidos*, Haggerty's *Yanqui* and *Mexicano* scum. Don Solomon's daughter was deeply moved by her lover's bravery, and she tacitly approved of the shooting of Richard Lingeman.

When Captain Haggerty finally turned from Lingeman's body and looked at Bart Braden, it seemed to the ramrod that the outlaw chief was on the verge of tears.

"How could ya do such a t'ing, Braden?" he said in a small, choked voice. "I was very fond of that lad. He was my friend." The big, fat man sniffled. Then he turned and walked away, out of the light of the campfire.

"They was, uh—real good buddies," Dan Cain told Bart Braden, with a leer that was in sharp contrast to the grief expressed by his leader. He was, as Braden found out later that night, first in line to succeed the late Richard Lingeman as Captain Haggerty's right-hand man.

The Texan nodded. "Yep, it's a damn shame, Cain. But if they was such good buddies, then that boy should've listened to ol' Haggerty."

As he turned to the lovely eighteen-year-old, Braden heard the sounds of muffled sobbing out in the darkness, just beyond the light of the campfire.

It was not the best way to begin his brief partnership with Captain Haggerty, the Texan reflected somberly as he drew Raquel close to him, seeking in the touch of her flesh the warmth that had suddenly gone out of his.

The ramrod knew that the Irishman never forgot, nor did he ever forgive a slight or an insult. He realized that he would have to be on his guard every moment of the day and night, from here on out. And as he smiled down at Raquel Mirabal, the Texan cursed himself inwardly, cursed himself for ever bringing the woman he loved to this nest of vipers.

"So they're a-gone to Hodgson, by Gad!" exclaimed John B. Loudermilk, smacking his fist into his palm. "So that's where them suckers go each time they disappears in these parts."

"They done give us the slip more'n once't in East Texas," T.C. Pritchett told Davy Watson and Soaring Hawk. "We never could rightly figger out where they'd gone to."

"It was like the ground done swallyed 'em up," Loudermilk added. " 'Twas the damnedest thing."

"Y'mean somebody's been puttin' 'em up in that town—Hodgson—all along?" the Kansan asked.

The two Texans nodded.

"Sure as a bear shits in the woods," rumbled Loudermilk. "An' now I know jus' who that someone is."

"Monte Tittiger, that's who," Pritchett added.

"Yep," agreed his partner. "Sum'bitch's the onliest one what's got the space to hide more'n a dozen horses. Couldn't be nobody else."

"How's that?" asked Davy Watson.

"Tittiger owns most of Hodgson," T.C. Pritchett explained. "Gen'ral store, saloon, hotel—"

"An' livery stable!" crowed John B. Loudermilk.

"Why, whenever Haggerty an' his Hellions come to town, ol' Tittiger must tuck their horses in his stable, an' board them owlhoots right in his damn hotel."

Pritchett nodded. "We never did trust that varmint nohow, did we, John?"

The burly ex-Ranger shook his head. "We sure as hell didn't. An' now we know why."

"We gonna go in after 'em tonight?" the Kansan asked, darting an anxious look at Soaring Hawk.

Pritchett shook his head. "We might mosey up there later on, an' size up the sit-chee-ayshun."

"But we ain't gonna do nothin' right away," Loudermilk added. "We gonna wait 'til sun-up. . .so's we can wish them boys a proper good mornin'."

"Where shall we go, Bart?" Raquel Mirabal asked her lover, snuggling up to him in the bed they shared in their room in Monte Tittiger's hotel in the East Texas town of Hodgson.

"I reckon we'll jus' sashay over to New Orleans, once't I done got ol' Haggerty his cows. An' then, I thought mebbe we might take ship to Califórnee."

"California," Raquel murmured excitedly, resting her head upon the Texan's chest. California was a place of romance and adventure to Don Solomon's daughter, a beautiful and abundant land whose Spanish names and heritage made her feel somehow as if she belonged there. And she *would* feel at home in California, the young *chicana* reminded herself, because so many of her people were there.

"Yes, I would like to go to California, Bart," she told her lover. "No one would know us there."

"Yep," Braden murmured, nuzzling her neck.

180

"I figger we could get us a right good start there, honey."

"You must be very careful," she told him, suddenly turning over and raising herself up on her elbows in order to face him. "I think these *hombres* are very dangerous."

"Yer right about that, Raquel," the ramrod agreed. "Meaner an' nastier varmints never trod the face of the earth."

"I don't trust *Capitan* Haggerty."

"Shows you got good sense. Why, he'd think nothin' of shootin' his own mother in the back, if'n there was somethin' to be got from it."

"And *you* shot his best friend," Raquel said accusingly.

The ramrod sighed. "That's a fact, honey. But you can be sure I ain't never gonna turn my back on Haggerty. Not never."

"I can't wait until we get out of Texas," Raquel murmured, her hand travelling down over his chest and belly.

"You ain't got long to wait," the ramrod told his love. "We jus' gon' pick us up a few cows, first."

"Oh, Bart," Raquel whispered in a voice which registered both surprise and delight. "You're already hard."

Braden twined his fingers in her thick, black hair. "Tha's jus' my way of payin' attention," he whispered back as Raquel's long, tapered fingers closed around his erect sex.

"You must show me more, *querido*," she whispered intensely.

"You like what we do, huh?" he asked as she

gripped him with both hands.

"Oh, yes," the young *chicana* answered in a voice that shook. Then she licked her full lips and began to lower her head. *"Oh, yes!"*

Braden's eyes widened suddenly, and he lifted his head off the pillow. And when he looked down, the ramrod was surprised to see his innocent young lover kneeling over him, her head poised above his groin.

She turned and shot him a hot, excited look. "I want to please you, Bart," Raquel whispered in a throaty voice. "I want to. . .kiss you." She stopped speaking and looked down to where she gripped his engorged sex in both her hands.

Staring in fascination at the beautiful and naked eighteen-year-old who hovered above him, watching her as carefully as a quail watches a goshawk, Bart Braden swallowed and then cleared his throat softly.

"I want to kiss you, Bart," Raquel repeated in a voice that shook with passion. "You have to. . .tell me. . .what to do." She cast him an imploring sidelong glance.

"Uh, well, Raquel," the ramrod began, shifting uncomfortably in the bed and looking straight up at the ceiling as he let his head drop back on the pillow, "you, uh, kinda got to go somewhat easy." He cleared his throat again. "It's like you, uh, don't gotta squeeze so hard, honey."

A flush began to suffuse the Texan's face as he said this, and he continued to stare fixedly at the ceiling.

"Oh," Raquel said in a small, alarmed voice, suddenly releasing her grip on his rod with the speed of a cowhand who had unwittingly picked up a rattlesnake instead of a branding-iron.

"But what else you was doin'," the ramrod went on, closing his eyes as he spoke, "was fine, honey. Right nice."

An instant later, he felt her fingers encircle his sex once more, lightly this time, followed by a resumption of the rubbing and stroking she had begun earlier.

After stroking his pole for some time, staring down at his groin with rapt attention all the while, Raquel finally spoke. "I want to. . .kiss you, Bart," she told Braden with gentle persistence.

"Uh-huh," he grunted, his face now the color of a slab of raw beefsteak. The Texan cleared his throat again. His eyes, opened once more, remained turned to the ceiling. "Main thing you got to remember," he mumbled, "is not to do no bitin'." For an instant he glanced down at his groin, and then quickly returned his gaze to the ceiling of Tittiger's Hotel. "That's very important, honey."

"I see," she whispered back, staring down at the prize in her hand like a little girl who has just been handed a kitten. "What else do I do, Bart?"

"Oh, well. . ." He cleared his throat for a long time. "You, uh, kinda take it in yer mouth, an'—"

"*All of it*?" she asked in alarm.

Braden's face was redder than ever. He closed his eyes. "Well, the top part, mainly," he mumbled.

"The *what*?" she asked, not fully catching his drift.

"The, uh, top part. The head."

"Oh. Is that what they call it?"

"Uh-huh. That's right, honey."

"Is that all I take in?"

"Well, if'n you feel you can take in some more—without gaggin' or nothin' like that, then I guess y'all can go ahead an'—you know." He opened his eyes, and then covered them with his forearm.

"What do I do then, Bart?" Raquel asked eagerly as she continued to rub and stroke him.

Again Braden cleared his throat. Then he heaved a deep sigh. "You, uh, sorta lick an'. . .suck." He cleared his throat once more. "You know," he said lamely, "stuff like that."

"Lick and suck," she repeated in a voice that registered a degree of puzzlement.

"Uh, yep," the ramrod went on. "Sorta like a deer at a salt lick. Or a kid a-pullin' on a lollipop."

"Oh, like *that*," she whispered, suddenly understanding what she had to do.

The ramrod sighed, his tense muscles finally relaxing. "Yep. That's right, honey."

As he closed his eyes once more, Bart Braden heard Raquel murmur something in Spanish, something he did not catch, the intonation of the words reminding the Texan of a prayer.

The young *chicana* thrust her hands down as far as they would go along his shaft, pressing into his groin and causing his *glans penis* to stand out well beyond her fingers. After that, she ran her tongue lightly and tentatively over his *glans*, and followed that by drawing back slightly as she moistened her full lips.

Then Raquel slowly lowered her head, parting

her gleaming lips and slowly taking the head of Bart Braden's sex in her mouth. Next, she began to do something that she had never been taught in the convent-school of Our Lady of Guadalupe.

Braden groaned, making a sound like a pole-axed steer dropping to the sawdust of a slaughterhouse floor.

As Raquel Mirabal pulled and sucked and licked like a two-year-old enjoying its first lollipop, she hummed happily.

The ramrod was breathing heavily now, snorting great blasts of air through flaring nostrils as the beautiful and passionate eighteen-year-old worked him over.

Her fingers traveled up and down over the shaft of his cock in light, spiralling runs. And her tongue started tremors in the pit of his groin, tremors which reached up his spine and penetrated his brain with waves that impinged upon his consciousness, causing the Texan to suddenly recall the image of an Oklahoma oil well about to blow.

As for Raquel, she was thoroughly caught up in the excitement of forbidden games, the convent-schoolgirl in her utterly fascinated by the dark joys of the flesh.

"Oh, God!" Braden moaned, his body suddenly stiffening as he was swept along by the irresistible tide of orgasm. "*Sweet Jee-sus*!"

Then the oil well blew, and Bart Braden grunted as a gusher of jism shot up through his ureter tube and streamed out into the ardent mouth of his beloved.

Raquel Mirabal's eyes went wide as her lover suddenly came in her mouth.

"*Ooooh—don't stop, gal*!" he cried out in anguish as Raquel suddenly froze with surprise. This was an aspect of "kissing" that the Texan had neglected to discuss with her.

"*Uuunh*," she grunted, recovering her wits almost immediately, and ministering once more to her writhing lover, after swallowing the first installment of his copious emission with a gulp.

The gusher flowed for some time, and the adaptable Raquel did her honey proud. And after she did, the grateful ramrod proceeded to inititate the eighteen-year-old further into the delights of oral sex, as he performed cunnilingus on her once more.

"Oh, Bart," Raquel Mirabal sighed as they lay together in the sweet aftermath of a night of energetic lovemaking. "It was wonderful. . .like nothing I have ever done before."

"You did right good, honey," the Texan murmured sleepily, planting a tender kiss on the nape of Raquel's neck and inhaling at the same time the delicate fragrance of her hair. And as he began to drift off to sleep, Bart Braden recalled Captain Haggerty's words:

"*Eat, drink and be merry, for tomorrow we shall die.*"

7

The End of the Trail

"I got to git that gal outta there afore ya start pumpin' lead into Tittiger's Hotel," the Kansan told the two former Texas Rangers.

"Aw, shoot," grumbled John B. Loudermilk. "That's gon' take the teeth out'n our surprise attack."

T.C. Pritchett nodded in agreement with this.

"Boys, I promised her daddy I'd bring 'er back in one piece afore I left New Mexico an' rid out after Bart Braden." He looked from Loudermilk to Pritchett, staring deeply into each man's eyes. "Gents, I give my word."

Loudermilk puffed up his cheeks and blew a whistling stream of air out between compressed lips. He raised his big hands in a gesture of helplessness and turned to his partner.

Pritchett sighed. "He done give his word to her daddy, John." There was a look of resignation upon his face.

The brawny man with the handlebar mustache sighed back. "Reckon we got to honor that, all right," he rumbled.

There was a relieved look on Davy Watson's face as he looked at his Pawnee blood-brother.

The four men were in the town of Hodgson, standing in the shadow of the livery stable owned by Captain Haggerty's old friend, Monte Tittiger, as they watched the hotel across the street.

The two ex-Rangers had chosen the stable as their vantage point because, with the outlaw gang's horses under their control, they would virtually have Haggerty and his bunch bottled up in Hodgson. Their original plan had been to encircle Tittiger's Hotel, and call for the immediate surrender of the desperadoes. And if no surrender was forthcoming, the Texans had decided to put the place to the torch, and shoot the outlaws as they fled the burning building.

"You gonna shoot them down jus' like that?" the Kansan asked, jarred by the cold-blooded scheme.

Both men nodded.

"These is the worstest scoundrels an' murderers in the whole state of Texas," Loudermilk explained patiently. "They'd only be dancin' at the end of a rope sooner or later, you can bet yer boots on that. An' thisaway, we's jus' makin' sure they don't escape."

"That's how we dealt with real bad 'uns in the Rangers," Pritchett told Davy and Soaring Hawk. "Jus' savin' the state time an' expense."

Davy Watson shook his head in disbelief.

"This ain't no instance of stringin' up some poor, innocent men," Pritchett went on. "Ain't no question but that all them boys in there is guilty—each an' every one, mind you—of the worstest crimes on the books. An' don't fergit, Bart Braden's a murderer, his own self."

188

"Shoot," Loudermilk growled. "That includes ol' Monte Tittiger an' his wife. Why, they's been accessories to the crimes of Haggerty's Hellions fer years now, I figger, 'cause they been shelterin' them boys—an' God knows what else."

Pritchett looked somber as he nodded a second time.

The Kansan had to admit it was basically the best way to deal with such a great number of desperadoes. After all, he and his companions were outnumbered four-to-one by the Haggerty bunch. But the presence of Raquel Mirabal in the hotel complicated things.

"Well, how d'ya propose to git that li'l filly out'n the hotel without wakin' up Haggerty an' all his friends?" asked Loudermilk.

"An' since Braden done ab-ducted her in the first place," added Pritchett, "it's fer damn sure he won't be far away from that gal."

Nodding at this, Davy Watson frowned as he recalled his midnight shootout with the Texas ramrod. Bart Braden was an extremely dangerous man, one who should never be underestimated.

"How you goin' git that gal out?" John B. Loudermilk asked once more. "Without ruinin' our little surprise?"

"It ain't gonna be easy," opined T.C. Pritchett.

The Kansan smiled at them grimly and then shook his head. "It ain't gonna be all that hard, neither," he told them.

Tap. Tap. Tap. . . .Tap. Tap. Tap.
A light-but-persistent knocking on the door

awakened Bart Braden. The ramrod was up on his feet in an instant, drawing on his trousers as he whispered, "Who is it?" and cast an anxious glance at the sleeping Raquel Mirabal.

"It's Monte Tittiger, Mr. Braden," a hoarse voice whispered back from the other side of the door.

"What d'ya want?" the Texan whispered as he drew his Colt .45 out of its holster at the foot of the bed, where his gunbelt was hung on a bedpost.

"Cap'n Haggerty wants to talk with ya, private-like."

By this time Braden was standing to one side of the door, with his gun held up at chest level. Recognizing the landlord's voice, the ramrod began to relax.

"Cap'n sent me up to ask ya to meet him downstairs," Tittiger went on beyond the door. "In the bar."

Braden darted a glance at the bed, and was relieved to discover that his beloved was still asleep.

"Hold on," he said, reaching for his flannel shirt with the hand that held the Colt .45, while he turned the doorknob with his free hand.

When the Texan opened the door, he was not prepared for the sight which greeted his eyes. There before him was Monte Tittiger, indeed, but with the barrel of a gun pointed up under his fat chin. And behind Tittiger, one hand on the Walker Colt and the other around the landlord's neck, stood the Kansan.

The only sound in the hall at that moment was Bart Braden's sharp intake of breath as he recognized the man who was hunting him. And before the ramrod could raise his own Colt, Soaring Hawk thrust the barrel of his Sharps rifle under the Texan's nose.

"Make one wrong move, Braden," the Kansan told his enemy, "an' Soaring Hawk here'll blow yer head apart like a overripe punkin what's been trod on by a plowhorse." His eyes were hard as Vermont granite, and his smile was as bright and sharp as a new Bowie knife.

"Well, I'll be hog-tied," Braden whispered in astonishment. "Watson—it's you."

"Goddamn right it's me, Braden," the Kansan replied in a steely whisper as he held out his hand. "I'm here to finish our business."

The ramrod bit his lip and darted a quick look over his shoulder at the still-sleeping Raquel Mirabal. Then, as he handed Davy Watson his Colt .45, Braden sighed and shook his head.

Davy took the gun, and then hit the ramrod in the chest with his forearm, thrusting him roughly back into the room. Then the Kansan entered, taking with him the sweating and red-faced Monte Tittiger. Soaring Hawk followed them, and quietly shut the door behind him.

"Git over by that wall," Davy told Braden, gesturing to his left with the Walker Colt. He thrust Tittiger roughly toward the wall. Soaring Hawk stepped forward and leveled his Sharps at the two men, motioning for them to raise their hands.

"Raquel," the Kansan called out in a firm, quiet voice. "Raquel, git up. We come to take ya home."

She fluttered her eyelids, stared at Davy Watson blankly for a moment, and then sat up with a start.

"*Dah-veed*!" she cried. "It's you!"

He raised a finger to his mouth, signaling for silence. "Git yer things on," he told her. "We're takin' you outta here."

Then Davy turned to Bart Braden. "Reckon you'll have to come, too. So don't try nothin', Braden. Y'hear?"

The Texan nodded. "I ain't 'bout to put Raquel in any danger."

"Well, now, I reckon it'll depend more upon you than upon me," the Kansan told Braden, as Raquel Mirabal donned her underthings beneath the cover of a bedsheet. And when he suddenly realized that the naked young *chicana* must have been sharing a bed with the ramrod, Davy Watson scowled.

"I ain't gon' give you no grief, Watson," Braden told him. "Not while Raquel's around."

"You damn well better not," the Kansan growled. " 'Cause I'm just itchin' to put a couple of bullets in you, Braden. But instead of that, I'm a-handin' you over to some fellas from the State Police. Seems they're right anxious to make yer acquaintance."

He smiled his Bowie knife smile. "Them boys is gonna be right glad to see you."

"*Dah-veed*!" Raquel Mirabal whispered urgently. "You can't—"

"Hush up, Raquel," Bart Braden told her, shaking his head as he turned to the young *chicana*. "The man got me fair 'n square."

Davy shot her a troubled look. "Hurry up now,

Raquel. We ain't got no time to waste."

In another minute they were all out in the hall, tip-toeing along the carpet, on their way to the stairs which led down to the ground floor of Tittiger's Hotel.

"My wife's upstairs," Tittiger whispered anxiously, turning to the Kansan. "What about her?"

Davy waved him out the door. "She'll just have to stay put fer now," he told Tittiger. "Le's go."

Then they were out on the street, heading toward the livery stable, with Tittiger in the lead, Raquel and Braden next in line, while Davy Watson and his Pawnee blood-brother walked several paces behind the ramrod, slightly off to each side of the prisoners.

They were halfway across the wide, dusty, main street of Hodgson now. From the rear of the little file, Davy could see John B. Loudermilk peering around the corner of the livery stable. The ex-Texas Ranger was nodding in admiration as he regarded the captors of Bart Braden.

Well, the worst is over, the Kansan told himself, smiling a wry smile as he shepherded Raquel, Braden and Monte Tittiger across the quiet street in the first light of dawn. *Now that we got Raquel back an' turned Bart Braden over to the State Police, all's we got left to do is deal with a dozen or so bad hombres that's a-sleepin' in Tittiger's Hotel.*

For an instant the Kansan thought about Monte Tittiger's wife. He wasn't especially looking forward to her being in the hotel when Loudermilk and Pritchett called for the surrender of Haggerty

193

and his Hellions.

Bam! Bam!

Suddenly two shots rang out, echoing loudly in the quiet street. They came from behind, from the direction of the hotel. Davy Watson crouched down and spun around, and as he did, the Kansan saw Bart Braden lurch forward and fall to the ground.

Bam!

Another rifle shot rang out, and the slug whined over Davy's head as he raised his Walker Colt and began to scan the front of Tittiger's Hotel. An instant later, he spotted the assailant: Captain Haggerty, his huge bulk thrust across the sill of an open window, was working the lever of a Winchester rifle as he sent another cartridge into its firing chamber.

Boom!

By the time that the Kansan had taken aim at the outlaw chief, Soaring Hawk had already fired his heavy-caliber Sharps rifle. The shot was a near-miss, blowing the window frame to smithereens just to the right of Captain Haggerty's head. The fat desperado cried out as a shower of splinters scored his face, and he ducked back inside the room.

At this point, Davy heard the sound of windows being raised. On both sides of the spot where Haggerty had opened fire, men with drawn pistols were leaning out of windows and beginning to bang away at the group in the street.

Bam! Bam! Davy's big Walker Colt bucked as he sent two shots at the gunman directly across from him. Then, without waiting to see whether or not his shots had found their mark, he spun around, still crouching, and came up behind the prisoners.

Raquel was kneeling beside Bart Braden, cradling his head in her lap. To his chagrin, as the Kansan ducked down beside her, he noticed tears streaming down the New Mexican beauty's cheeks.

"Git over there, Raquel," Davy ordered, pointing to the livery stable where John B. Loudermilk was firing at the hotel with a carbine.

Whi-i-ing! A bullet whined, and then spanged just behind Raquel Mirabal, sending a jet of dust into the air as it plowed into the ground.

Davy's eyes widened as he watched the young *chicana* shake her head stubbornly. Out of the corner of his eye, he could see Monte Tittiger rush by, his back prodded by the barrel of Soaring Hawk's rifle.

"Hah! Got that sum'bitch!" John B. Loudermilk cried exultantly as he lowered his rifle, smiling grimly at the hotel window where Arthur Danforth, the Virginian outlaw, dropped his pistol out the window and followed it a moment later, pitching down to the street.

Bam! Blam!

The shooting continued as Davy Watson squatted down beside the fallen Bart Braden and looked Raquel Mirabal in the eye.

"Judas Priest, you're stuck on this galoot!" he exclaimed in amazement as he looked down at the Texas ramrod.

Bwi-i-ing! Another bullet spinged in the dust, not more than a foot away from Raquel Mirabal. And as the Kansan stared down at the bloodstained front of Braden's flannel shirt, he heard the answering roar of Soaring Hawk's Sharps.

The sound of shattering glass filled the air. Braden grimaced in pain as he tried to speak.

"Git Raquel outta here, Watson," he said.

"I won't go unless we take him along," Don Solomon's daughter told Davy in a firm voice.

The Kansan nodded, realizing that taking Braden with him would be the best way to ensure Raquel's cooperation. He leaned over, grabbed hold of the lapels of Braden's denim jacket, and pulled him to a sitting position.

At the same time, in back of Tittiger's Hotel, a door creaked open and two armed men rushed out into the daylight.

Blam! Blam!

Two shots rang out, and the last of the men to leave the hotel was flung against the wall. He cried out loudly, clutched his right side with both hands, and sank to his knees in the dust.

"*Fernando*!" Eufemio Salcedo cried when he turned and saw his dying younger brother. Then the pot-bellied desperado spun around and leveled his gun at the copse of cottonwood trees which faced the back of the hotel at a distance of more than a hundred feet.

Salcedo fired off two answering shots before the second volley from the cottonwoods cut him down.

In the copse of trees, his rifle resting on a sturdy limb, T.C. Pritchett looked up and nodded, smiling in grim satisfaction.

By this time a third figure had appeared at the door. Michael Shaughnessy, the ruffian from Hell's Kitchen, pegged three wild shots at the ex-Ranger, cursed loudly, ducked back in the hotel, and slammed the door shut.

"*Get him! Shoot the bastard dead*!" Captain Hagerty roared, foaming at the mouth as he leaned out the shattered window and began blasting away at Bart Braden, whom the Kansan had just slung over his back.

"Skeedaddle, Raquel!" Davy called out, tottering for a moment under the ramrod's weight as he straightened up.

From a series of windows adjacent to Captain Haggerty's, the Hellions began to pour their fire out onto the street.

Bam! Bam! Whi-i-ing! Blam! Boom!

"*Die, ya filthy, murtherin' bastard*!" Haggerty roared in a paroxysm of insane rage, still banging away at the man he hated above all other men. "A loife fer a loife! Now I'll avenge me poor Dickie!"

The Kansan sighed with relief as he saw Raquel Mirabal disappear around the corner of the livery stable, where John B. Loudermilk continued to pepper the outlaws with his carbine. And as he lurched around the corner himself, Davy heard the reassuring boom of Soaring Hawk's Sharps, as the Pawnee covered him from one of the building's front windows.

Raquel Mirabal cried out in anguish as Davy Watson staggered into the stable and dumped Bart Braden onto a pile of hay.

"Oh, he's hurt badly!" she gasped, kneeling at the ramrod's side.

The Kansan scowled and shook his head as he made his way to a window. And as he did, Davy stepped over the recumbent form of Monte

197

Tittiger.

"What happened to him?" he called out to Soaring Hawk as he knelt beside the window.

"Nothing," the Plains Indian called back. "Too busy to guard him, so I hit on head with rifle."

"Cap'n! Cap'n!" Squint Ryerback yelled in alarm, "The damn hotel's on fire!"

"Oh, Jay-sus!" the beefy, red-faced Irishman moaned. "What? *This* hotel?"

Across the street, the Kansan's eyes went wide as he saw flames leap up from both sides of Tittiger's Hotel, with accompanying clouds of smoke which began to billow up past the windows of the wood frame building's second story.

"Good work, T.C., ol' hoss!" John B. Loudermilk roared exultantly. "Whoopee! We gon' smoke out them varmints now!"

"Fire an' brimstone!" Doc Doucette called out as he ducked into Captain Haggerty's room. "It's spreadin' like blazes, Cap'n—on account of that damn wind what's a-comin up from the east!"

"Holy Mary, Mother of God!" the Irishman swore, turning to the powerful graybearded old man. "Now, where's the Salcedo boys? Did they get over across the street?"

Doucette shook his head. "Nope. Some jasper was layin' fer 'em in the cottonwoods. Done plugged 'em both."

"Jay-sus Chroist!" the outlaw chief screamed in a voice shrill with rage and frustration. "It's that bloody fookin' Braden! He put the jinx on me, by God!"

Just then Eli Satterthwaite, the big, bald-headed

198

man with the patch over his eye, bolted into the room.

"The buildin's goin' up like kindling!" he called out in a voice that shook. "They got us trapped like rats in here. What we gonna do, Cap'n?"

The Irishman's face was redder than ever, and his jowls danced to the pulse of his anger. "Get me Tittiger's woifes!" he ordered, turning to Michael Shaughnessy.

"Right y'are, Cap'n," the New York City ruffian grunted as he rose to his feet.

A moment later he cried out in a high-pitched, whimpering voice and collapsed on the floor, a bullet from the Kansan's Walker Colt in his right temple.

"*Dead-Oiye!*" Haggerty screamed. "*Dead-Oiye, where are ya?*" The fat desperado slammed the butt of his rifle down on the floorboards. "Them bastards over there is after pickin' us off one-by-one. Git over here, an' give 'em what for!"

The scrawny little man with the oversized Adam's apple and the Bill Cody hair scurried into the room on all fours, a sharpshooter's Henry rifle in his left hand.

"I-I-I was tryin' to get the sum'bitch what f-f-fired the house in my sights, Cap'n," Dead-Eye Dan Bates explained. But he hung too c-c-close to the buildin'."

"How'd the place go up so fast?" asked Doc Doucette.

"M-musta done s-s-soaked it with k-k-kerosene whilst we was all asleep," speculated Bates. Then he crawled to the window, giving the body of Michael Shaughnessy a wide berth.

"Git over here an' pop off a couple of them divils across the way," Haggerty told him impatiently.

"I-I'll do m'level best, sir," said the scrawny desperado.

"Who's coverin' the back of the bloody house?" Captain Haggerty asked in sudden alarm.

"Fritzie an' Puma's watchin' it, Cap'n," Bates said out of the side of his mouth as he scanned the front of the livery stable.

"Who else is left?" Haggerty asked.

"Dan Cain an' Jimmy Blount, far's I can tell, Cap'n," was Squint Ryerback's reply.

"I'll go get Monte's ol' lady," Doc Doucette boomed as he began to crawl out of the room.

Just then, Dead-Eye Dan Bates fired off a brace of shots.

Blam! Blam!

"*Ooooof!*" grunted John B. Loudermilk, his carbine flying into the air as one of the slugs from Bates' rifle shattered his left forearm. The brawny ex-Ranger ducked behind the livery stable wall, sagging against it as he drew his sixgun.

Back in the burning hotel, the sharpshooter had moved his rifle, and was in the process of lining the Kansan up in his sights.

"Here comes Number Two, Cap'n," Bates whispered, exhaling gently as his finger tightened on the trigger.

Boom!

Thunder broke across the street as Soaring Hawk's Sharps rifle detonated. And with a sound much like that of a melon smashing under the blow of a blacksmith's hammer, the sharpshooter's head burst apart under the impact of the slug from the Pawnee's weapon, spattering the room and its occupants with bits of brain and bone and flesh.

"Yahoo!" Davy Watson yelled. "You got that sum'bitch, my brother!"

The back door of the hotel creaked open once more, and Jimmy Blount, the captain's mute manservant, jumped out and began to dash for the shelter of a buckboard that stood no more than twenty feet away from the building.

Blam! Blam! Bam! Bambam!

Two shots rang out from the cottonwoods, followed an instant later by three more from the opposite direction. And as Jimmy Blount clutched at his gut and fell to the ground, T.C. Pritchett uttered a strangled cry and threw up his rifle. A bullet had caught him in the eye, entering his brain. By the time that the ex-Texas Ranger hit the ground, he was dead.

"That takes care of you, *amigo*," Dan Cain muttered as he drew back from the window and lowered his smoking pistol. "Now we can get outta here."

"Mister Watson," John B. Loudermilk called out in pain and sadness a few moments later. "I think they done got ol' T.C. I don't hear his rifle no more. We got to keep the back of the hotel covered, or them varmints'll all break loose. Now, I'm shot, an' losin' lots of blood, so you or yer buddy'll have to go over there."

"All right," Davy Watson called out. "Cover me, you two."

Fortunately for the Kansan, great sheets of flame leapt up before the front of the hotel as he

201

made his perilous sprint across the wide street. This, in combination with the heavy covering fire laid down by Soaring Hawk and Loudermilk, enabled him to skirt the building and reach the cottonwoods unobserved.

"Bedad, I've got a woman here," Captain Haggerty roared out the window when the flames had momentarily subsided. "An' I'm goin' to use her to shield me when Oi come out of this place, so give way."

"That don't cut no ice with us, Haggerty!" the brawny ex-Ranger roared back. "That ol' slut is as guilty as you are, an' I ain't got no qualms 'bout lettin' her have one 'twixt the eyes, neither. Yer a dead man, anyway, so whyn't you jus' let 'er go, an' come out a-fightin' like a man?"

"Oh, Captain—don't let 'em shoot me!" blubbered Monte Tittiger's wife, a tall hatchet-faced blonde.

"Cap'n, the back is clear!" Dan Cain called out as he dashed into the room. "The stairs is startin' to burn, an' if'n we don't shag ass outta here right away, we'll roast like wieners."

Boom! The Sharps rifle cracked across the street, and Dan Cain suddenly shot back through the open door, the latest victim of the hawk-eyed Plains Indian.

"Down, lads!" the captain cried. "Oh, bejaysus," he moaned, gnawing on a knuckle. "Whoever's got that big gun is an even truer shot than poor ol' Dead-Oiye."

Haggerty turned back to the window, taking care not to expose himself, and cupped his hands over his mouth.

"All right, whoever y'are," he yelled. "We're

comin' out with our hands up. Give me an' my lads a minute to get downstairs, an' we'll send Monte Tittiger's auld lady out ahead of us.''

"Come ahead—but come out with yer hands held high,'' John B. Loudermilk yelled back in a voice shot through with weakness and pain.

"Now, lads,'' Haggerty whispered to his men. "Collect the others that's still aloive, an' we'll go stormin' out the back door, trippin' loike the hammers of hell.'' He waved them out impatiently. "Go on, we ain't got much toime.''

"What about woman?'' he was asked by Puma the Apache, once he had crawled out of the room. The big Indian was holding Monte Tittiger's wife, who by this time was pale with fear.

"Bring the auld bag along,'' Haggerty growled as he lumbered toward the stairs, covering his face as a sheet of flame leapt up before him. "It can't hurt to have her wit' us.''

Several seconds later the back door of the hotel flew open, and the surviving outlaws burst out and headed for the safety of the cottonwoods. . .unaware that the Kansan was there, waiting for them.

The first one out was Squint Ryerback, who made for the trees as if the devil himself were on his heels. Next came the giant German, followed closely by Eli Satterthwaite and Doc Doucette. After them came Puma, dragging Tittiger's whimpering spouse with him. And last, but certainly not least, his jowls trembling as he ran, came Captain Daniel Patrick Haggerty.

The Kansan lined the foremost outlaw up in his gunsight and waited patiently. As he aimed T.C. Pritchett's Winchester, the Kansan steadied himself against the very same limb which the fallen ex-Texas Ranger had used. The man's corpse lay at Davy Watson's feet.

Squint Ryerback was now only twenty-five feet away.

Blam!

The Winchester cracked, and the little man shot backward, rolling over in the grass to land in a heap, his scrawny neck bent at an impossible angle.

Thirty feet behind him, the three big men skidded and floundered as they clumsily attempted to stop dead in their tracks.

Blam! Blam!

Eli Satterthwaite screamed and spun around, his pistol flying through the air. The bald man with the black eyepatch clawed at his throat, as he sank to his knees and uttered wet, gurgling sounds.

Old Doc Doucette dropped to the ground and began to fire back at the unseen rifleman in the cottonwoods. Fritz Oberst looked from the trees to the burning building, and then back to the trees. Firing a brace of shots, the giant lumbered off, heading for the shelter of the buckboard that stood behind the hotel.

Blam!

The Kansan's slug caught the German in the small of the back, causing him to straighten up and stop dead in his tracks. Then he turned stiffly and began to fire in Davy's direction.

Davy fired off one more shot before he ducked behind the tree. Oberst and Doucette had finally located the Kansan, and were now making it hot for him.

In the meantime, Haggerty and Puma, who continued to drag Mrs. Tittiger with him, sought shelter behind the buckboard.

Boom!

There was a sudden, thunderous roar, and the Apache was knocked off his feet, never to rist again, dragging the screeching, terrified woman down to the ground with him.

Captain Haggerty dove for the ground and rolled over until he collided with Monte Tittiger's wife. Then, just in time to avoid taking Soaring Hawk's second bullet, the fat desperado thrust the woman in front of him.

Bang!

Splinters flew through the air as a slug blew apart a branch not six inches above the Kansan's head. Oberst was on his knees in the grass now, bracing his gun in both hands as he took careful aim at Davy Watson, who swore and did his best to reload the Winchester before he got shot.

Boom!.

The German giant shot forward and flopped on his face without uttering a sound. Soaring Hawk's shot had blown the top of the man's head off.

The Plains Indian, once he had been stalemated by Captain Haggerty, ducked back around the house, intending to deal with the other surviving desperadoes. Then he saw Oberst about to shoot his blood-brother, and quickly dispatched the German.

"I give up," boomed Doc Doucette, flinging his pistol up into air and rising stiffly with his hands held above his head. "Don't shoot an old man."

"You just come forward 'bout ten paces, Pop,

205

an' then stay put,'' Davy ordered the big old man. Then he turned back to the burning building and was surprised to see Soaring Hawk facing Captain Haggerty, as the latter held Tittiger's wife in front of him as a shield and aimed his gun at the Pawnee.

Haggerty had rushed around the corner just as the Pawnee was about to reload his Sharps. Soaring Hawk tossed the gun aside and went for the scalping knife in his belt, but the Irishman shot him before he could draw it.

Bam! Bam!

Captain Haggerty fired two shots at the Pawnee, one of which knocked him to the ground. And then the outlaw chief moved in for the kill, thrusting Tittiger's wife aside as he started forward and drew a bead on the fallen Indian.

''Judas Priest!'' Davy Watson exclaimed as the billowing smoke suddenly hid the captain and Soaring Hawk from view. It was impossible to aim at anything now, and certainly too far away for him to run there in time to save his blood-brother. The only thing the Kansan could do was to wait and pray.

''Now, ya red bastard!'' Captain Daniel Patrick Haggerty cried out in exultation as he aimed his gun at the fallen Pawnee, who lay unconscious on the ground before him.

Crack! Crack!

Two short, sharp bursts rang out in the smoky air. Captain Haggerty dropped his gun, howled like a banshee, and began to claw at his back. His eyes were already glazing when he looked around and saw Monte Tittiger.

The captain's former accomplice held a smoking

Derringer in his hand. "How dare you treat my wife that way!" Tittiger said to Haggerty, just as the latter gurgled and fell on his face in the grass.

As the smoke cleared, Davy Watson saw Monte Tittiger chuck his Derringer onto the grass, turn toward him, and raise his hands in the air.

"I'm unarmed, mister," Tittiger called out as his wife ran to his side. "An' you don't have to worry 'bout Captain Haggerty no more."

"Jus' keep 'em up, an stay where you are," the Kansan called out to the man who had shot the Irish desperado. Then he took one last look at the corpse of T.C. Pritchett and stepped out of the shelter of the cottonwoods.

"Git over with them two people," Davy told Doc Doucette, once he had made sure that the old man was not carrying any concealed weapons. And after searching Tittiger and his wife, Davy knelt down beside he body of his Pawnee blood-brother.

To his relief, the Kansan discovered that Soaring Hawk's wound was not a fatal one. Captain Haggerty's bullet had caught the Plains Indian in the upper part of his right thigh, sending him to the ground. And when he fell, Soaring Hawk had banged his head against a rock.

When he had bound the now-conscious Pawnee's wound, Davy left him propped up in the buckboard, with a pistol trained on the prisoners. And as he started toward the livery stable, the Kansan wondered why John B. Loudermilk had not joined him.

Tittiger's Hotel was blazing away like a Fourth of July bonfire, and as Davy Watson made his way across the street, its bright and flickering light illuminated the front of the livery stable.

He saw a pair of boots sticking out from behind the wall as he rounded the corner of the building, boots he recognized as belonging to John B. Loudermilk. And when he turned the corner, the Kansan saw the ex-Texas Ranger sitting slumped against the wall of the livery stable, a pool of blood around him, his head on his chest, and his hat lying on the ground.

Apparently the shot that Loudermilk had taken from the rifle of Dead-Eye Dan Bates had not only shattered his forearm, but opened an artery as well. The brawny state policeman had bled to death.

When he went inside the building, Raquel Mirabal raised her head from Bart Braden's chest and shot Davy Watson a stricken look. The Kansan realized that the ramrod, the man who had stolen Raquel from her home and caused so much death and devastation, was dead, too.

"I loved him," Raquel said in a small voice. "*Ay, Dios*," she wailed, brushing the dead Texan's cheek with trembling fingers. "*Bart, mi corazón!*"

The Kansan bent over, took the stunned *chicana's* arm, and helped her to her feet.

"C'mon, Raquel," he whispered. "I'm gon' take you home to yer daddy."

Then I'm gon' home to Kansas, he told himself as he led her out of the livery stable. *An' this time, I ain't lettin' nothin' stop me.*